You Don't Need an Enemy

YOU DON'T NEED AN ENEMY

by

Richard Martin Stern

72-02353

Charles Scribner's Sons • New York

For D.A.S. and M.E.E., with love.

1

It was the daily maid — Miss Lucy Carruthers tolerated no sleep-in help — who discovered the body that bright Santo Cristo morning. Her screams for help in both Spanish and English reached well beyond the adobe walls of the Carruthers estate. Will Carston, who lived a little farther down the Camino, was first on the scene.

Will was seventy-five, a poet (Pulitzer Prize), a scholar (his monumental work on the Spanish Land Grants of the area was nearing completion), and what was once called a gentleman of means. He and Miss Lucy had feuded for years, but Will, unlike some, did not believe in carrying his feuds beyond death. Standing, looking down at Miss Lucy's body sprawled without dignity amidst a great deal of dried blood on the polished tile floor, Will said, "I'm sorry about this, Lucy. I wish you well wherever you have gone." Then he went to the telephone and called the police.

In Santo Cristo, and sometimes in its environs as well, homicide was the particular business of Lieutenant Juan Felipe Ortiz, usually known as Johnny. He was a middle-sized man, lean and wiry, with straight black hair in a crew cut. Dark eyes in a dark face, and although the white teeth flashed often, the eyes rarely seemed to smile. Old Ben

Hart, who was popularly supposed to fear neither man nor devil, had been heard to say, "You study on Johnny Ortiz, and you'll see why the word Apache used to scare folks half to death."

Johnny drove a police car into the graveled turn-around of the Carruthers house, got out, and took a few moments to look around with enjoyment.

As age was measured in Santo Cristo, the house was not old, a mere hundred years or so; but it had been planned with care to fit into its surroundings, and with its adobe walls, its *vigas,* its multiple chimneys, and its low silhouette, it could have been built almost any time within the last three and a half centuries.

It was set in eight and one-half acres of walled privacy, with a sweeping view of the towering mountains nearby, in May still snow-capped, as well as of the sloping mesa to the south, dotted with piñon and juniper, stretching to the broken horizon a hundred miles away.

Within the walls there was green lawn and flower color in profusion — faintly pink apple blossoms, the deeper pink of flowering crab apple, golds and whites and purples of iris, white and deep-lavendar of lilac, all neatly tended, expensively groomed. Miss Lucy Carruthers believed in perfection. Or had.

It was not, Johnny reflected, the kind of location you associated with violence, which was a ridiculous thought, because violence, like gold, was where you found it. He walked to the front door.

Will Carston met him. "The maid actually found the body," Will said, "but the shock undid her." As it had not, obviously, undone Will. "I poured a hooker of Lucy's brandy down her throat and by now she may be coherent. She's in the library." Pause. Then, in a matter-of-fact tone, "Lucy's in here." He led the way.

2

Miss Lucy lay on her back. She was fully dressed even to short white gloves, one of her famous no-nonsense flat felt hats, and a light sweater against the chill of a May evening. Her large handbag, unopened, lay on its side at her feet. For a small woman, Johnny thought, Miss Lucy had contained and lost a remarkable amount of blood.

Johnny stood for a moment contemplating the scene, the pleasant sunny room, the quietly expensive furnishings, the tile floor undoubtedly polished daily lest in this country dusty footprints showed. He hunkered down and squinted sideways against the light of the windows. A few faint traces of footprints were there, and these he examined for some time. Then he stood up. "We'll wait for Doc Easy before we touch her," he said. He glanced again at the traces of footprints and made a mental note to ask the maid about her cleaning routine. To Will he said, "You're the nearest neighbor. I don't suppose you heard anything last night?"

Will shook his head. "Sid Thomas was over. We played some cribbage. We talked." He seemed unaffected by the body that lay at his feet, and he seemed to sense that Johnny watched his unconcern with interest. "I drove an ambulance in France in the 1914-18 war," Will said. "What squeamishness I had I lost then. Permanently." Pause. "About last night — my hearing is not what it was. Neither is Sid's." He glanced down. "I assume she was shot, but I heard nothing." He looked again at Johnny. "For the record," he said, "Lucy Carruthers and I were not on the best of terms."

Johnny nodded and smiled faintly. The feud was notorious.

"But I am not a violent man," Will said, "and I possess no firearms, and I am in no way responsible for this." Pause. "Lucy was not on the best of terms with quite a few people."

Johnny nodded again. The way he heard it, Miss Lucy Carruthers had spent a long and energetic life in combat with almost every person she had ever met. Wealthy eastern spinsters and widows were no rarity here in Santo Cristo and almost without exception they tended to make their presence felt, but Miss Lucy, heiress to a Boston fortune founded on the eighteenth-century triangular rum-slaves-molasses trade, had thrown her weight and her wealth around with abandon. There was simply no counting the toes on which she had trodden, nor the ribs that had felt the sharp thrust of her bony elbows. *Nil nisi bonum* . . . "I'll bear it in mind," Johnny said.

Will seemed to hesitate. "If you want me," he said, "I'll be at home." He strolled out into the sunshine.

Johnny found his way to the library. The maid, Spanish-American, sat uncomfortably in one of the over-stuffed chairs. She had her handkerchief rolled into a damp ball and she worked at it with her fingers. "Juanita Otero, *señor.*" She spoke in rapid Spanish. "I came into the house through the kitchen as I always do. I went into the living room to dust, and, *Madre de Dios!,* there was the *señorita!*" Enormous dark eyes stared at Johnny's face. With a hand that shook, the girl crossed herself, and then sat silent.

Johnny leaned against the large desk. "You are here all day?" He too spoke in Spanish.

"Sí, señor."

"Until what time?"

"Until the *señorita* needs me no longer."

"Last night?"

"Last night, *señor,* I left before seven o'clock. The *señorita* had only tea. She wanted no dinner."

"She was going out?"

4

"I do not know, *señor.*"

"She is wearing a hat, gloves, a sweater," Johnny said.

The girl began to cry. Johnny waited with that built-in patience that was part of his heritage until the tears stopped. Then, "You went in to dust the room?"

"*Sí, señor.* It is the first thing I do each morning."

"And the floor?"

The girl seemed more relaxed now; talk of routine soothed her. "With a dust mop I do the floor each morning, *señor.* Once a week Juan, the gardener, waxes and polishes the floor."

So far, Johnny thought, so good. He switched direction. "Yesterday," he said, "did Miss Carruthers have any visitors?"

There had been several: the librarian from the local college, no doubt interested in donations to the library; the chairman of the Opera Guild of which Miss Lucy had been a vigorous and contentious member; the curator of the museum; and — "Who?" Johnny said, and although nothing showed in his face, his mind was suddenly on edge.

Juanita hesitated. She was quite aware that she was walking on very thin ice because all the world of Santo Cristo knew that the Lieutenant Juan Felipe Ortiz and the woman scientist Cassandra Enright from the museum were, as the Anglos said, *that way* about each other. On the other hand, Juanita dared not withhold any information whether it had meaning or not. It was doubtful if in any event the lieutenant would have her staked out on an ant hill, as his ancestors had been fond of doing, but Juanita was not prepared to take the risk. "The *señorita* Doctor Enright, *señor,*" she said. "She came here in mid-afternoon."

"Did she see Miss Carruthers?" Johnny was unaware

5

that he had switched back to English. What had Cassie wanted here?

"*Sí, señor.* They — quarreled. I was in the kitchen, but I could not help but hear."

"What did they quarrel about?" Johnny's voice was soft.

"I do not know, *señor.*"

"How do you know they quarreled?"

"Their voices, *señor.* They were raised in anger." The girl's hand could not stay still; her fingers worked at the balled-up handkerchief. She was again very close to tears.

"Did you hear anything they said?" Johnny watched the girl closely.

"*Sí, señor.*" It was a small voice, filled with reluctance. "The *señorita* Doctor Enright asked why the *señorita* Carruthers did not drop dead. Many people, the *señorita* Doctor Enright said, would be much happier if she did." Pause. "That was all I heard, *señor.*"

Bastante, Johnny thought, more than enough.

Doc Easy had arrived by the time Johnny sent the Otero girl home. Doc was an easterner in his late sixties, retired from Boston practice and unhappy in retirement. "Something about the air out here," he had told Johnny once. "It won't let you just sit on your ass doing nothing. So I might as well do what I know best how to do."

He said now, "She was shot. You guessed that already." He was standing, looking down at the body and shaking his head. "I've seen a fair number of gunshot wounds, but I haven't seen many that tore a body up like this."

Cassie, Johnny thought — damnit, he'd talk to Cassie later. Right now he had work to do. "Shotgun?" he said.

"No." Doc was definite. "We'd find pellets. This was one bullet, neat little hole in front, and a good share of her back carried away."

"Large caliber?" Johnny said.

"Maybe." Doc was hesitant. "A .45 does an awful lot of damage, but if it strikes much bone it may not even go all the way through. This one did, and kept right on going." Doc paused. "Like one of those hand guns, that .357 Magnum — I remember reading that a shot went through the back of a car, through the back seat, the front seat, through the driver of the car, and into the engine." He was silent for a moment. "Just a guess."

"Lieutenant." A patrol car cop, on hand if Johnny needed him. "What about this?" He was standing at a large sofa, pointing down at one of the cushions. "There's a hole in it."

Johnny picked up the cushion. He felt it carefully with his fingers. "And," he said, "there's a bullet inside." He shook his head slowly. "Some days you can't win for losing. Then you get a break like this." He handed the cushion to the patrol car cop. "State Police lab," he said. "Saul Pentland, nobody else. Have him call me with whatever he can make out."

He turned back to Doc Easy. "She wasn't too tall," he said. "Somebody holding a hand gun waist high might be shooting a little down, somebody taller than she was. My height, say." Or Cassie's height in boots, he found himself thinking; and tried to turn the thought off. "If that's the right bullet in the cushion."

Doc Easy said, "How many shots do you think have been fired in this room?" He studied Johnny's face. "Something bugging you?"

"I hear voices," Johnny said.

2

Johnny Ortiz was thirty years old, the product of a half-Anglo and half-Spanish-American father, name thought to be Ortiz, and an Apache mother; educated at reservation school, and, *mirabile dictu,* at State University. Apache Athabascan was his native tongue, but he was equally at home in both English and New World Spanish.

When he wanted to he could lay on a Leo Carillo Spanish-American accent; but he only did this at times when internal pressures required that either he make a mockery of himself or let himself go in violence. And since Cassie Enright, these times had been infrequent. He headed for the museum and Cassie now.

She was in her tiny office, with Chico, the puppy Johnny had given her, lying at her feet. Cassie was *café-au-lait* in color, and once she had told old Mark Hawley: "I'm a black chick with a go-go dancer's carcass and a head filled to the eyeballs with anthropological erudition. Where am I going to find a man who'll take all of me seriously?" Well, here he was, walking in with blood in his eye. Frowning, Cassie leaned back in her chair and waited.

Johnny perched on the corner of her desk. "You saw Lucy Carruthers yesterday, no? What about?"

He was Johnny Ortiz, and there was and had always been in him this brutal directness, this black-and-white-no-gray-allowed approach, his own standards set impos-

8

sibly high and everyone else expected to measure up. ("I scrambled out of a hut, goddamnit, don't tell me you never had a chance.") "I saw her, yes," Cassie said. "She wants to cut off the funds for the Cloud Mesa dig, and she wants me to drop everything and go down to Mexico with her because she doesn't want to be cheated if she buys some pottery, and she's knifing Carlos in the back with the other museum trustees, and —" Cassie stopped. In a calmer voice she said, "She is just being Lucy Carruthers, which is another word for obnoxious. Does that answer your question?" She too had her pride.

"She is also dead," Johnny said, "shot sometime last night." He paused. "And you were heard, *chica,* asking her why she didn't drop dead and make a lot of people happy."

Cassie took her time. At her feet Chico stirred restlessly and made a small questioning sound. Cassie ignored him. Her eyes had not left Johnny's face. "Am I your prime suspect?" she said at last. "Is that what you're trying to say?"

He could not explain it, because motives and feelings were too hopelessly entwined. If he had not cared for her as deeply as he did, he would have dismissed the remark Juanita had overheard as merely one of those things someone said in temper. But because she was Cassie, his Cassie — at least he had come to think of her as *his* Cassie — she had to be like Caesar's wife, totally above suspicion, and that was where the rub came in. *"Chica,* don't you see —?"

"No," Cassie said, "I don't see. I detested the woman, and I don't care who knows it."

"That isn't very bright," Johnny said. "It's almost as if you're asking for trouble."

"Maybe I'm not very bright. Had you thought of that?"

9

"Chica —"

Cassie said, "I can think of a dozen people in this town who would like nothing better than to hear that I'm suspected of shooting Lucy Carruthers. They'd say, 'I told you so. You take a black chick and educate her and she gets uppity and there's no telling what she'll do if she takes a mind to it.' "

Johnny clung tight to his temper. *"Chica —"*

"Thanks very much," Cassie said slowly, distinctly, "for telling me I'm on your list. I won't run away. I promise." She picked up a paper from her desk and began to read. Dismissal. Reading, she found, was difficult. Her eyes were blurred with tears.

No one paid any attention to the automobile that was parked on the Camino a few hundred yards above the Carruthers' drive until a patrol car, passing the spot for the fifth or sixth time that day, stopped to investigate.

The car, a Chrysler New Yorker, local license, was empty. The glove compartment was locked and the keys were gone. The patrol car driver copied down both license and automobile serial number, and radioed them in to headquarters. In about three minutes he had his answers:

The automobile was registered in the name of Miss Lucy Carruthers, address: the Camino. From the National Crime Information Center computer in Washington there was a negative report – the automobile had not been reported stolen.

Johnny, notified, sent a man out with the car keys from Miss Lucy's purse to drive the car to the house. The car would not start. It was out of gas. "So," Johnny said, and began to see a little light; not much, but some. He was still trying to put Cassie out of his mind.

Saul Pentland called from the State Police lab. The

bullet had been shot, as Doc Easy guessed, from a .357 Magnum, specifically a Colt Python, and that, too, rang a kind of bell. Colt Pythons were not all that common. Johnny went in to see Sergeant Tony Lopez. "You had a burglary report —"

"Amigo," Tony said, "I am up to my ass in burglary reports."

Johnny was aware of it. There were times, he thought, when it seemed that crimes were cyclical or even epidemic: there might be a sudden rash of knifings, and then those would die away to be replaced by hit-and-runs, or wife-beatings, or riots and window-breakings in protest over God only knew what. Right now, and for the past few weeks, burglaries had sprung into prominence. "The one I mean," he said, "listed a Colt Python along with other stuff stolen."

Tony nodded wearily. "Fellow named Hastings, Don Hastings, sculptor, Anglo of course, apparently loaded – a missing wrist watch listed at $650, that kind of money." He was watching Johnny's face. "You know him?"

"I know him," Johnny said, and walked out.

Johnny had never been to Don Hastings' studio, but he knew where it was – up Arroyo Road not quite as far as Cassie's house. The studio was of adobe, with a large north light no doubt giving a splendid view of the nearby mountains. A brick walk led down from the road to an enclosed patio filled with Hastings' sculpture, wood in bas-relief, stone figures in the ancient Mexican manner, two cast bronze figures in a curvilinear style wholly different from all the others. As he knocked on the carved front door, Johnny decided that experimental would be the word for Don Hastings' art. To Johnny's mind this kind of experimentation smacked of dilettantism.

Hastings was home. He answered the door in his

11

working clothes of blue jeans, disreputable sneakers, and a soiled sweatshirt. He was a big blond man, with a ferocious mustache and pale blue eyes. Johnny held out his identification, but Hastings did not even glance at it. "I know all about you, lieutenant," Hastings said. His tone seemed to indicate that he didn't particularly like what he knew.

"May I come in?" Johnny said. "I'd like to talk to you."

"About what?"

"Your gun that was stolen."

Hastings hesitated. Then he stepped back and held the door wide. "Why not? Be my guest."

It was a large studio room, and the north light did give a spectacular view of the mountains. As in the patio, Hastings' sculpture was on display. Johnny glanced at the figures idly. Hastings watched him as if he waited for reaction, and then Johnny saw why. On a table in the corner was a bronze statuette perhaps two-feet tall, a nude female figure, meticulously modeled, pure realism. Johnny walked over to it and studied it closely. It was, as he had thought, Cassie to the life, every lovely curve and attitude.

He turned slowly. Hastings was watching him. Johnny said, "About that gun." Was there a hint of a smile behind the ferocious mustache, a brief flicker of triumph? For the moment, no matter. "You kept it where?"

"Where I keep all my guns." Hastings gestured to a far corner. "In the gun case."

Johnny walked over to look. In the case was a 30-06 sporting rifle with a scope mounted; an overpowered .22, also with scope; a 12-gauge over-and-under Browning; and a double-barrleed 16-gauge Parker. There was, Johnny reflected, a lot of money tied up in those four guns.

Hastings said, "I keep the hand guns in the drawers." He opened one drawer. In a walnut case, velvet lined, was a

Browning custom .22 automatic target pistol; and beside it in a sheepskin case, a Ruger .22 automatic with a bull barrel. Hastings opened the other drawer, and drew in his breath with a little hiss.

There were three hand guns in this drawer: a .45 Colt automatic; a S&W .38 target revolver; and, lying on its sheepskin case, a Colt Python, .357 Magnum.

Johnny looked at Hastings. Hastings picked up the Magnum as if it were hot. He swung out the cylinder and looked at the number stamped on the gate. "37529," he said. He looked at Johnny. "It's mine." Pause. "You aren't going to believe this, lieutenant, but it wasn't here yesterday."

"It's the one you reported stolen?"

"It is the one that *was* stolen, lieutenant. Somebody is playing tricks, and I don't like it. Goddamnit, a man's property isn't safe any more." He stopped. He looked down at Johnny. "You don't believe me, do you?"

"Maybe," Johnny said. "Maybe not." He held out his hand. "I'll need that gun for a little while."

"Why?" The belligerence had returned. "It's mine. I even have a New York license for it."

Johnny's hand was still outstretched. "You may not be so happy it is yours," he said. "A woman was shot and killed with a .357 Magnum, a Colt Python, last night. We'll want a shot fired from this for comparison." He took the gun gently from Hastings' hand and held it by its checkered walnut grip while he got out his handkerchief and wrapped the gun carefully. He looked up then. "By the way, did you know a Miss Lucy Carruthers?"

Hastings opened his mouth and closed it again in silence. He took a deep breath. Some of the color had gone out of his face. "She's the one?" He waited for no answer. "Oh, migod," he said. "Aunt Lucy!"

3

Cassie had a caller that afternoon. "Billy Joe Harmon, ma'am, and I am right pleased to make your acquaintance." Tall, wide through the shoulders, with a firm, practiced handshake. "By trade," he said, "I'm an automobile salesman, ma'am, but you might say I'm here because of my inclination." He smiled easily. "I like to work with boys." Specifically underprivileged Spanish-American boys, who, left alone, tended to gravitate into trouble. "You see, ma'am, their problem is lack of interest, and I try to stir things up a little for them."

Highly laudable, Cassie thought, but she failed to see where she fitted in. She said as much. That scene with Johnny still depressed her.

"Why, ma'am, you underestimate yourself," Billy Joe said. "I attended your slide lecture on that place in Mexico, all those ruins, and what their culture must have been like before Columbus and all those Spanish came busting in, and I tell you, ma'am, I was spellbound. All I could think was how much the boys would get out of hearing you talk and seeing your slides and finding out just how great some of their people were in those days. It's an Anglo world, ma'am, and these boys need a sense of pride in their origins."

True enough, Cassie thought, and of universal

applicability; everybody, herself included, needed something sturdy to lean on. Until Johnny had walked in that morning her own sense of pride, based solidly upon his affection for her, had been strong and satisfying. Now, suddenly, everything seemed spoiled. "If you really think they would be interested, Mr. Harmon," she said, "I'll be happy to talk to them and show them the slides."

Long after Billy Joe, elated, had gone off to see about setting up a date, Cassie just sat and stared at the wall and wondered what had gotten into her that morning to react as she had. Temper to match temper? Defensive because she realized she should not have said what she did say to Miss Lucy? Oh, damn, damn, damn! The telephone interrupted her soul-searching. She picked it up and spoke her name.

"Cassie baby, I need your help." Don Hastings, at the moment seeming like a voice out of the past. "That damn Indian of yours is out to scalp me."

Cassie frowned at the wall. "What in the world do you think I can do?"

"Stop by for a drink after work," Don said, "and at least talk to me." Pause. "Or have I suddenly turned contagious?"

"Don't be silly," Cassie said. "I'll stop by." What else could you do when someone asked for help?

At the State Police lab Saul Pentland fired Don Hastings' Python into a box filled with insulating material. Saul was a big man, an ex-offensive tackle for the Dallas Cowboys. In his smock he always reminded Johnny of a white bear. Now, pawing through the box, he said, "Sometimes the hardest part of the whole thing is finding the damn bullet in all this stuff — ah, there it is. Come out, you little rascal.

His big hands were deft at the comparison microscope, setting the bullet from the pillow in Miss Lucy's house in juxtaposition with this new one. He twiddled the knob and grunted in satisfaction. "No doubt," he said. "Same gun. Have a look for yourself."

So far, so good.

Cassie, drink in hand, sat in Don's studio. Over on the corner table stood that statuette she had posed for nude — and why not back then? She supposed Johnny had seen it and recognized it, and what had he thought? Today, of all days? Don't answer that, she told herself, and tried to concentrate on what Don was saying.

It was a threnody. "It's almost as if somebody is out to get me, which makes no sense at all. You read about these things, but you don't actually believe them." He drank deep. It was not his first drink.

Cassie, watching, listening, seemed to detect undertones of near-panic, as if his reaction to pressure was they-can't-do-this-to-me, pure lament without force. And this was strange, because in their relationship before Johnny had entered Cassie's life, it had always been the man, Don Hastings, who held all the cards: male, Anglo, well off if not downright rich, and very much a man of the world. Now he seemed to have shucked off his outer covering, and, like the football player without his enormous shoulder pads, stood before her shrunken to less than life-size. "It can't be that bad," Cassie said.

"Somebody stole my gun," Don said. "Then he used it. Then he put it back. What does that add up to you?"

Cassie set her drink down. "You don't even know yet that it was your gun that shot Miss Lucy."

"It was. I know it." Gloom and depression produced their own unhappy certainty. "And Aunt Lucy, too. Migod."

"I didn't know she was your aunt."

"Well, she was. And she more or less controlled the purse strings, and we didn't get along very well —" He spread both hands. "Now do you see how it looks? I'm her next-of-kin, and what do you think your Indian will make of that?"

Cassie's eyes went automatically to the nude statuette. Hastings nodded. "Yes, he saw it. I thought it would be pretty funny if he did, he's so damned sure of himself, but now I wish I'd hid it."

Johnny sure of himself? Was that how it looked to the world? Cassie had a sip of her drink and wondered if she, too, appeared confident and serene. Incredible. *"Cui bono?"* she said. "Who benefits? And you inherit? Is that what you're thinking?" It was exactly what he was thinking; the answer showed plain on his face. "Where were you last night?" Cassie said.

"Out."

Cassie shook her head. "Not good enough."

Belligerently, "Look, don't you —" He stopped. Cassie had stood up. "Where're you going?"

"I think you'd better get a lawyer," Cassie said. "There's nothing I can do." She had started across the studio when the knock came at the door. She stopped and looked at Don.

"Here we go," Don said, and went to answer the knock.

It was Johnny, of course. He looked at Cassie, and nothing showed in his dark face. To Hastings he said, "Your gun killed her. Do you want to tell me about it?"

"I've already told you. The gun was stolen. Then it was returned. I don't know any more about it than that."

Johnny appeared wholly at ease, the hunter concentrating on a trail, caring not where it led, merely confident that in the end he would find his quarry and drive him into a corner from which there was no escape. Merciless was the word. "If it was returned, as you say," he said, "then it had to be last night, doesn't it?"

"I wasn't here." Mistake. Hastings tried to recover. "I mean —"

Johnny moved in pitilessly. "Where were you?" Pause. "At the Carruthers house?"

An animal in a trap, Cassie thought, bewildered and frightened. Oh, damn, damn, damn! "He was with me," she said. "At my house." She met Johnny's eyes squarely. "Does that satisfy you?"

The room was silent. Johnny's eyes went to the statuette, then back to Cassie. After a long pause, "For the moment," he said, and walked out. The door closed solidly.

Don Hastings let his breath out in a long sigh. "Cassie baby —"

"Oh, shut up!" Cassie said. "Go run your money through your hair." She walked to the door and opened it. The sound of Johnny's car was already fading. Cassie walked alone out into the night.

4

The daily maid, Juanita Otero, recalled to the Carruthers house, calmer now, went through room after room in the presence of Sergeant Tony Lopez. "I see nothing missing, *señor.*" She shrugged expressively. "But sometimes it is difficult to tell if something is gone."

Agreed. Tentative conclusion: no burglary.

"I'm not sure," Johnny said, "although it could be." He had put Cassie out of his mind, or almost. He was pretty sure she was lying about being with Hastings last night, but at the moment proof was not possible. What Johnny thought of Hastings because of Cassie he kept to himself, pushed into a tiny corner of his thoughts where it could fester and wait. In the meantime, he was leaning over backward to give Hastings every break he could, and if that made no sense at all, why, Johnny was not going to put up an argument; it was merely the way it was. "Look at it this way," he said to Tony. "Miss Lucy was going out, probably had an engagement somewhere — we'll see if we can find out about that. Hat, gloves, sweater, handbag. She got the car started and drove out a couple of hundred yards and the car stalled. Out of gas. She walked back and let herself into the house to phone for help. She surprised somebody. What does that add up to?"

Tony Lopez was no fool, and his confidence in himself was both wide and deep. On the other hand, he had found that arguing with this crazy Apache Johnny Ortiz was usually a pretty discouraging business. The man had visions, or seemed to, and there were times when he plucked things out of the air when nobody else had even heard the sound of wings. "You tell me, *amigo.*"

"It could have been a burglar," Johnny said. "But a burglar carrying that kind of cannon?" He shook his head. "And the cannon that belonged to the woman's nephew? Coincidence?" Again the head shake.

Tony Lopez had advanced the tentative conclusion of no burglary. Now he was not at all sure. That was the kind of thing this *brujo* Ortiz did to you. "Look," he said. "Hastings and Miss Carruthers — they're both loaded, lots of stuff in their houses, they're a good hit. They ——"

"Wait a minute," Johnny said. He stared at the wall. Damn Cassie, anyway; she kept interfering with his thoughts. He got things clear at last. "Where was Hastings the night his house was burgled?"

Tony sighed. It was this oblique approach that got you. You covered all the facts, ran down all the details, and what the man wanted to know was the one point that seemed completely irrelevant. "I don't know. Just out." Tony shrugged.

Johnny said, "You pick a place that looks like a good hit. You case it. Then what? You hang around and wait until the owner goes out at night and you go on in? But you don't know how long he'll be gone. He might come back in five minutes, and there you are."

"Like the Carruthers woman." Tony nodded.

"No," Johnny said. "Let's think of that a different way. Somebody knew she was going out and would be gone for some time. Maybe the somebody even arranged it. What about that? But he hadn't expected her to run out of

20

gas. The night Hastings went out and came home and found he'd been burgled — had he arranged the date; or had it been in the paper that he was going to be somewhere, maybe to give a lecture or something; or had somebody *asked* him out, and if so, who?"

Tony thought about it, and the more he thought the less he liked the implications.

"One other thing," Johnny said. He was on a trail now, and although it was very faint, and possibly led nowhere, he was concentrating again, as he had not really been able to concentrate since that first talk this morning with Cassie. "It used to be," Johnny said, "that the kinds of things stolen from houses here were what you'd expect kids to steal — money, portable radios, portable TVs, clocks, stuff they could either use themselves, or maybe peddle to other kids at school, no?"

Tony shook his head. "Not any more. Now it's $650 wrist watches, diamond rings, silverware — if it really was gone like he says, a $160-$175 Colt Python, that's what's reported stolen these days."

Johnny nodded. "And if it was stolen, that gun, then it was also returned, and what does all that add up to? Kids? What would they do with a diamond ring, an expensive wrist watch? Why would they *return* the gun?"

Tony wished they had never started talking. He sighed and said a few short words in Spanish. Then, "You're talking about an organization." It had been there all along, of course, right under his nose, and maybe Tony hadn't seen it because he hadn't wanted to see it. "You get the damndest ideas," Tony said. "The trouble is, this one makes sense."

Chico followed Cassie around the house, when she came home from Don Hastings', like a small four-footed

shadow; and when at last she sat down, he sat too and stared up at her mournfully, working his black nose in an attempt to search out the cause of her obvious unhappiness.

The little dog had been the beginning of a major change in her life, a first breach of the wall of loneliness she had constructed between herself and the world. And then through that breach had come Johnny. *Had* come. Had he walked back out now? Well, she thought, at least Chico remained, and she could talk to Chico. "In the first place," she said, "I don't like telling lies."

Chico studied her with his brown eyes and considered the matter. He gave the floor a couple of tentative thumps with his tail.

"What I ought to stick to," Cassie said, "is anthropology. I know my way around there. Don't look so happy, because I am miserable." (Simple truth.)

She thought of calling Johnny, which was, of course, the sensible thing to do, and telling him that she had not been with Don Hastings last night. But she had a sniggly feeling that Johnny knew it already, and there were few humiliations greater than those of pointless confession. And where had Don Hastings been, anyway? Hadn't you better give that some thought, Cassandra?

She got up from her chair and went to the record player, contemplated briefly, and then selected Mozart, the *Jupiter* Symphony — music to think by. She went back to her chair.

Miss Lucy Carruthers had more or less controlled the purse strings, Don Hastings had said. Don had never lacked for bread, but perhaps his plenitude was dependent on his behavior in Miss Lucy's eyes? A new thought, and where did it lead?

A most unpleasant character, Miss Lucy; bother the

22

admonition to say nothing but good of the dead. A cantankerous, opinionated, overbearing, contentious woman possessed of a circuit rider's sense of self-righteousness, and powered by a bloodstream that must have been, in Cassie's private opinion, ninety per cent pure adrenalin and ten per cent vitriol. What would have been her opinion of, and her attitude toward, her nephew?

For one thing, Don Hastings was large and male and not unattractive, and Cassie had noticed that Miss Lucy tended to pull her punches just a little when she gave battle to large male, not unattractive, adversaries. Old Ben Hart, for example, was almost, but not quite, without blemish in Miss Lucy's eyes. A plus there for Don Hastings in his relations with his aunt.

Then, too, Don was a sculptor, and if he was no Rodin or Michelangelo, his work was careful and even competent. And Miss Lucy had always viewed herself as a patroness of the arts. Another plus for Don.

On the debit side, Miss Lucy's views of life tended toward the rock-ribbed-New-England-coast-Calvinist way of thought, and high on her list of thou-shalt-nots were intemperance, sloth, and lechery, and here Don did not come out so well.

Don drank, sometimes to considerable excess; he enjoyed pot; at one time or another he had, as he had told Cassie, taken a whirl at acid and peyote and other assorted goodies, just, of course, to see what their effects might be. Miss Lucy's attitude toward these diversions, if she knew of them, would have been less than tolerant.

Don was lazy. When he wanted to work, he worked hard and long, even in a kind of frenzy. But he lacked the self-discipline of the real artist, the professional; nor was he driven by Miss Lucy's frenetic fanaticism; and so he tended for long periods to sit, placid and contented,

23

nibbling at his own brand of lotus. Miss Lucy must, from time to time, have been irked by this kind of inactivity. "Let us, then, be up and doing . . ." without doubt had been woven deep into the fabric of Miss Lucy's upbringing.

Lastly, Don liked girls and devoted himself to their pursuit. Along Arroyo Road, where sexual activity took a multiplicity of forms, and excesses were far from uncommon, Don's appetites were viewed with a tolerance they would not have been accorded elsewhere, and particularly not up on the Camino in the large house where Miss Lucy dwelt. Santo Cristo being the echo chamber it was, word of Don's proclivities must at some time or another have reached Miss Lucy's ears.

Face it, Cassie told herself, relations between aunt and nephew must have been tenuous, and at times downright strained. Today, watching Don, listening to his laments, she was convinced she had seen into his being and found it weak. Charming and weak; how often the two went together. But along with weakness, and charm, there could also be viciousness, as from time to time she had had occasion to discover — and now she was seeing matters in a new and different light.

The first side of the Mozart ended. Cassie got up and turned the record and went back to her chair. She sat quiet for a little time, allowing her thoughts to roam at will. She did not like the direction they took.

"Chico," she said at last, and the little dog's head came up at once. "It is distinctly possible, Chico," Cassie said, "that your mother goofed badly. Stop thumping your tail. This is serious. I thought he was scared, bewildered, unable to cope with any kind of pressure. And Johnny is implacable." She paused. "But maybe what I was looking at was an act for my benefit, and the reason he didn't tell me where he was last night is that he couldn't think fast enough."

24

Another pause. "Maybe that gun was never stolen in the first place. It did seem odd that along with the wrist watch, and the cuff links, and the silver that was taken, one gun would go too, and not all the others, which are worth a bundle. What do you think of that?"

Chico showed a length of pink tongue and wiggled his rump ingratiatingly.

"Well, I don't like it a bit," Cassie said, and meant it. "Maybe there was the burglary, and Don took that opportunity to say the gun was stolen, because from that night on he had in mind to get Miss Lucy off his back." Could she really see Don Hastings, dilettante, bon vivant, lecher, as Mack the Knife? How in the world would I know? she asked herself. That's Johnny's province, not mine. And again she was tempted to call Johnny, and again she shrank from almost certain humiliation.

She stood up at last. "Stay here, Chico," she said, "and guard the house. I'm going pub-crawling. If Don was anywhere innocent last night, somebody in this incestuous community will know."

5

Johnny was also on the prowl and for the same reason. There were times when he deplored the fact that Santo Cristo was what it was, ingrown, its tail in its mouth; almost anyone's appetites, weaknesses, and indulgences known by someone and widely broadcast. But there were other times, like this one, when living in a goldfish bowl had its advantages, especially for a cop.

"Show me what you like, and I'll tell you what you are." Johnny couldn't remember who had said that, but it was true, and reversible. Johnny had a fair estimate of what Don Hastings was; his likes, then, were not difficult to deduce: not for Don Hastings the bowling alley, the evening movie (unless an X-rated Guild flick was playing), the Peek-a-Boo Lounge (topless entertainment amidst the deafening clamor of hard rock), or a quiet night climb up Sun Mountain to watch the moon rise. Don would be a gregarious fellow, and he would prefer to be amongst his own kind.

Johnny started at the foot of the Arroyo Road stretch devoted to bars, coffee houses, and restaurants sandwiched between art galleries and craft shops. As it happened, Cassie was starting down from the top of the same stretch.

Johnny's first bar was El Tecolote y El Gatito. It was run by a young woman named Sam, and it was small,

26

crowded, and decorated with murals on the plaster walls showing the Owl and the Pussycat in various situations. There were tiny tables and wooden chairs with raffia seats. Candles in bottles provided the only light. When Johnny reached the bar, Sam came down behind it shaking her head. "Oh, God," she said pleasantly, "the fuzz. What have we done?"

Johnny showed the white teeth. "I wouldn't know." He liked Sam. She was what she was and made no bones about it; and if her tastes were not Johnny's, who cared? He kept his voice casual. "Has Don Hastings been in lately?"

Sam drank black coffee, nothing else during working hours. She reached for her mug, sipped at it, and then set it down, her eyes never leaving Johnny's face. Slowly she shook her head. "You don't ask questions just for fun. Suppose I say he has been in recently?" She paused. "Say like last night? What then?"

"I'd check it out, Sam, and I wouldn't like it if I found you'd had me on."

Sam nodded. She smiled faintly. "I bet you would at that, and you know what, I wouldn't like to be in your black book." She shrugged her big shoulders. "I haven't seen Don in two, three days. That's straight."

"Thanks, Sam."

Sam nodded. She said, "You are *mucho hombre*, Johnny, *con cojones*. Nothing there for me, but I like quality wherever I find it. Drink?"

Johnny showed the white teeth again. He shook his head. "I've got a long road, but thanks." Out into the cool night. Scratch El Tecolote y El Gatito.

Scratch, too, El Portal, which was a coffee shop with chess tables and (by airmail daily) copies of the *New York Times* and *Variety*.

Johnny drew a blank at Eddie's, the restaurant; and

27

at the Torremolinas bar next door. At El Rincón, bar with discotheque, crowded, smoky, noisy, he picked up some information tinged with malice. "Don baby was in here last night," the bartender said. "He was stoned, and he had a chick with him ——"

"What chick?" Johnny's face showed nothing. Cassie? Inside he felt drawn up tight as a fiddle string.

The bartender shrugged. "Who knows? They come and they go and there's not much point trying to find out a name because you'll probably never see them again. Just a chick, an Anglo with a Texas accent."

Some, but not all, of the tension within him began to ease. Johnny said, "Stoned. On alcohol?"

The bartender grinned wickedly. "At a guess, I'd say on pot and alcohol both, which I'm told is not a very good combination. I let him have one drink and then told them both to get lost. Don baby can get mean when he's stoned."

Johnny said, "What time did they come in, and what time did they leave?"

The bartender thought about it. "They came in like about eight. They left maybe half an hour later."

"Going which way?"

The bartender jerked a thumb. "Down the road."

Toward the Camino, Johnny thought; maybe that was significant, maybe not. "Thanks." He walked out and stood for a few moments in thought.

Don had not been with Cassie; that was point one, more important than all the others put together. All right, he'd settle that with Cassie herself later.

If the bartender was to be believed, Don had been stoned, and when he was stoned he could be mean. Mean enough to kill? It was Johnny's opinion that nobody could predict with any degree of certainty what anybody would

28

do in a tight situation. And if Don, stoned, had gone to see Miss Lucy, the situation would have been tight. Miss Lucy's views on intemperance were well known.

Don and the girl had gone down the road, not up; *away* from Don's studio, and *toward* the Camino, on which Miss Lucy lived. And he, Johnny, had already covered the spots down the road, without result, so, presumably, Don and the girl had not been simply on a pub-crawl.

Enough, he told himself; even cops had to eat and sleep. Tomorrow was another day, and there were things to do, the first of which was to have a talk with Cassie.

If he had stayed where he was for another ten minutes he could have had his talk with Cassie right then.

She was not alone. At Fred's Place a little farther on up the road, she had acquired an escort: Billy Joe Harmon. "Why, ma'am, I do hate to see a lady all by herself at night. Somehow, it just don't seem fitting, and I'd be proud to walk with you wherever it is you're going."

It sounded, Cassie thought, like something out of a bad TV Western; but, then, Billy Joe himself, auto salesman and guider of youth, didn't seem quite real either. Still, going in and out of bars by herself was not the most pleasant of occupations. Offer accepted.

Until they reached El Rincón, they had found no trace of Don Hastings. "I wonder if I know him, ma'am," Billy Joe said. "A big fellow with blond hair and a mustache?"

"That's the one," Cassie said, "and I wish you'd stop calling me ma'am." She was smiling. "You couldn't very well mistake me for Southern aristocracy, now, could you?"

"Ma'am — excuse me," Billy Joe said. Then,

smoothly, "What I was going to say was that I could mistake you for a queen without any trouble at all, none."

How gallant could you be? "Not 'your majesty,' either," Cassie said. "Cassie will do very nicely." In an old-fashioned, still somewhat unbelievable way, he was sweet. "El Rincón is next."

The bartender said, "Why all this sudden interest in Don baby?"

Cassie said, "Someone else has been asking?" She turned on her smile, the full treatment. "Who might that be?" Of course, of course, Johnny would want to know; and that meant he had not believed her story. "And Don was here last night?" She listened. "Do you know who the girl was?"

"Like I told the fuzz," the bartender said, "they come and they go."

.   At El Tecolote y El Gatito, "This is the last bar," Billy Joe said. "I'd be honored if you would let me buy you a drink, ma'am — Cassie."

They sat at the bar and Sam brought her coffee mug to join them. Sam had had her eye on Cassie for a long time, and while she didn't think she would ever get anywhere with her, it was always pleasant just to be close. Even in a blouse, sweater, wheat Levis, and boots, her working costume, Cassie was a female to admire.

Billy Joe talked about his one-man youth movement. "It isn't exactly a club, but we do have an old shed we've fixed up, with a punching bag and horseshoes to pitch outside and I got a radio with green stamps, that kind of thing just to give the kids something to do."

Sam was looking at the creamy flesh in the open throat of Cassie's blouse. "Sounds great," she said.

"Maybe I talk too much about it," Billy Joe said, "but it's the kind of thing that gets to you, if you know what I mean."

"I think so," Cassie said. She was smiling. He *was* sweet. And unreal. Now why did she think that? To Sam she said, "How did Johnny seem? Angry about anything?"

"Honey," Sam said, "I never can tell what that man thinks. He has angry eyes, and then he shows you those white teeth, and for all I know he's measuring me for a scalping knife. Another drink?"

Billy Joe walked Cassie all the way to her house up at the head of Arroyo Road. "I'm not sure it's safe out alone at night," he said. "You being a woman, and all." He paused. "I'd purely hate to see something happen to you."

"So would I," Cassie said. "But nothing has yet." Not quite true. There were those two boys waiting for her that one night. Levis and boots helped a lot. Still, if you lived in constant fear of what might happen to you, you might as well be dead, for all the enjoyment life could give. She opened the door and Chico came rushing out. "My protection," Cassie said. "Or he will be when he's a little larger. Will you come in for a nightcap?"

"I thank you, but no." Pause. "You be careful, ma'am — Cassie. You hear? And if the police are interested in what that Don Hastings was doing last night, then I don't think maybe you ought to be too. If something shady is going on, you don't want to be mixed up in it, now, do you?" Another pause. "Good night, ma'am. I thank you for your company."

6

Old Ben Hart came to town these days no oftener than he felt he had to. Too many people coming and going, too many cars and too much traffic around the plaza, too many *turistas,* too much of just about everything.

Ben was well into his seventies, a great bear of a man, customarily dressed in Levis and boots and a plaid shirt, in summer cotton, in winter wool, with the sleeves turned back on his blacksmith's forearms. He owned some forty-five thousand acres of mesa land sprinkled with piñon, juniper, chamisa, cholla, prickly pear, and grama grass; and he had leased another twenty thousand acres on which his cattle also roamed and grazed. He had one stream that rarely went dry, and he had sunk enough deep wells to keep his stock tanks filled. When he did come to town, as this morning, he drove his Cadillac, a great dusty monster, and State Police made a point of looking the other way.

He had two missions this morning. The first was to pay his respects to Miss Lucy Carruthers, or at least to find out when respects could be paid. He had had no illusions about Miss Lucy. In Ben's opinion her abrasive exterior covered a heart of granite. On the other hand, Miss Lucy had been a fixture in Santo Cristo for quite a spell now, and Ben purely hated to see his contemporaries go. Also, he had had a considerable regard for Miss Lucy's no-

nonsense attitude in a fracas; she always reminded him of the old bare-fisted days when a man clawed and scratched and fought for what he wanted, or to protect what he had. So, good luck, Lucy, and good hunting wherever you are.

The second mission was different. You thought you knew every inch of your land, and by and large you did. But just yesterday, over toward Cloud Mesa, which was adjacent to Ben's holdings, a silly calf had worked its way into some brush and cactus and gotten itself hung up and was bawling its fool head off when one of Ben's men came along in a pick-up and stopped to see what he could do about rescuing the beast. He got himself skinned up in the process – cholla and prickly pear would as soon tear your hide off as produce pretty blossoms for you; sooner – but he did get the calf out. More important, he almost broke a leg falling into what looked to be an abandoned kiva that just might, Ben thought, tie in with Cassie's dig up on Cloud Mesa, and he thought she ought to know about it. He liked Cassie. If, by God, he'd been thirty-five years younger . . .

The museum was open when Ben parked in the plaza. He walked in, and met Johnny Ortiz coming out. Ben caught the glint in Johnny's eye. "You look," Ben said, "like you'd take on a rattlesnake and give him first bite. What's up, son?"

Johnny had no comment.

"Cassie in?"

Johnny shook his head.

"Where is she?"

"I don't know," Johnny said. "I'll find her later." At Don Hastings' studio again? He was behaving, he told himself, just like any other moonstruck swain – and the knowledge did nothing for his composure. He walked out to his pick-up and drove over to see Doc Easy.

There was no point in Ben's going inside: if Johnny said she wasn't there, then she wasn't there. But it was strange, because Cassie was unusually prompt and conscientious. Ben got into the monster Cadillac and headed up through town for the Camino. Will Carston would know what arrangements were being made for Miss Lucy's remains.

He took Arroyo Road as the most direct way to the Camino, and then, as long as he was on it, he decided to drive on up to Cassie's house. It wasn't a hunch; Ben didn't believe in hunches. It was just that in this country over the years habit became ingrained: if somebody was not where he was supposed to be, you generally went out looking for him because it was big country and things did happen and a man, or a woman, could be in bad shape unless somebody turned up with aid. Not here in town, of course, but still, the habit was too strong to be ignored.

Cassie's car was in the carport. That was the first thing. The second was the whining, whimpering sound the puppy was making inside the house, and after that Ben wasted no time.

The front door was locked. Ben threw his shoulder against it twice, and on the third try the lock broke and he went through. The living room was a mess, a table, chairs overturned, a lamp lying shattered on the gleaming brick floor. The puppy, on three legs, rushed to him whining. "Cassie," Ben said. "Cassie!"

The sound he heard in answer was faint, like the mewing of a kitten. It came from the bedroom, and Ben went through the doorway, a charging bear.

Cassie was there, lying across the bed, wearing what was left of a nightie. There was blood on the white pillowcase, and more blood dried on Cassie's cheek. Her lips moved, but only the faint mewing sound emerged. Ben touched her bare back gently with one big hand. "All

34

right, honey," he said. "It's all right. Just lie still." Then he went to the telephone.

Johnny was with Doc Easy. "The time of Miss Lucy's death," Doc was saying, "say somewhere between eight and nine. She had tea and toast, the maid says, at about quarter of six to six o'clock, so we have a pretty good fix."

He was on a trail again, so he could push Cassie at least out of the forefront of his mind. Eight to nine, Johnny thought; and the barkeep had said that Don Hastings and the Anglo chick with the Texas accent had left about eight-thirty. It could fit. "Doc," he said, "could pot and alcohol be an explosive mixture?"

Doc hesitated. "It would depend." Pause. "On the — I hate to use the word, but there it is — the personality involved. And on the quantities of each taken, and how fast they were taken —"

"But it *could* be explosive?"

Doc sighed. He nodded. "It could be, I think. Not really my field, but —" He spread his hands.

"That's good enough," Johnny said. "Thanks." He started for the door. The phone began to ring, and he stopped. Tony Lopez at headquarters knew where he was. But the call wasn't for him.

Doc's face went blank, and his voice was without expression. "All right. Don't move her. I'll come." He hung up. He looked at Johnny. "Maybe you'd better come too." No point in pulling punches. "Somebody broke in on Cassie Enright last night. She's been beaten. Badly. Maybe raped." For a moment Doc was not sure Johnny had heard the words, but he had.

"Let's go," Johnny said, and that was all.

Later, Johnny was never entirely clear about the events of that morning. A cop did well, he knew, to keep

35

himself uninvolved lest feelings got in the way of thought; but there were times when logic became irrelevant, and then a man reacted as his core and his heart dictated.

He did hold himself in check even after he saw Cassie's blood-stained face and the bruises that were on her body, her closed eyes and her total *helplessness;* and heard the shallow painful sound of her breathing. The temptation was to break something, anything; but he made himself stand still. When the ambulance came, he stood by while Doc Easy supervised the operation of getting Cassie off to the hospital and then started for his own car. "Coming, Johnny?" Doc said.

Johnny shook his head. At the moment he did not trust himself to speak. He walked back into the house, where Ben Hart waited. Ben had Chico on his lap and was exploring one of the little dog's legs with gentle fingers. Chico whimpered and trembled, but made no effort to get away. "Offhand," Ben said, "I'd say he's been kicked. Hard. I think this leg's broken." He stood up, the little dog in the crook of one arm. "I'll take him to the vet." He paused. "You?"

"I'll be here for a while."

Ben nodded. "And then?"

"Some people I want to talk to."

Ben nodded again. "Don't do anything rash, son." As he walked out he thought that his advice was just about as effective as a fart in a whirlwind. To the puppy he said, "Just hang in there, little sizer. We'll get you fixed up." The Cadillac roared off down the dusty road.

Johnny stood for a long time in the wreckage of the living room, and the feeling was strong, inescapable, that the scene was wrong. He squatted beside the smashed lamp base and without touching it examined the switch. The switch was on. So? He rose slowly. "How the hell do I

36

know yet?" he asked himself and the room at large; sheer anger, nothing more. But, by God, he was going to find out.

He started for the bedroom door, and there he stopped, and hunkered down again, squinting sideways at the polished floor. Footprints, dusty and faint, almost invisible, coming from and going to the bedroom. One of them was a pointed-toe shoe, small built-up heel – the kind of Beatle-boot thing half the Spanish kids in town wore. Kids? To do this kind of job on Cassie? He straightened again and walked into the bedroom.

He knew it well, as well as he knew, or had known, the woman who lived in it. There were latched screens on the windows, and no indication that the latches had been forced. He walked into the bathroom. Here too the single window was untouched. That left the spare room, which Cassie used as an office and a catch-all. There were two windows. One of them was still open an inch or so at the bottom, and here beneath the window he could just make out another of those faint, dusty footprints, and, yes, other footprints as well. He hunkered down to study them.

It was a long time before he rose again to his feet and, automatic movement, dusted his hands on his thighs, his eyes never leaving the floor. Three sets of footprints, to his eyes as individual as different faces. And one set of footprints he had seen before – yesterday morning on the gleaming tile floor of Miss Lucy Carruthers' house. Ponder on that, Juan Felipe. He walked slowly, thoughtfully back into the bedroom.

There was a fine two-gray-hills Navajo rug on the floor, which was a pity, because rumpled as it was, it showed no discernible footprints. So back out into the living room to hunker down and examine with minute care the area just beyond the doorway. One pointed-toe footprint going into the living room, another, the same foot in the same shoe, coming back. And, of course, all the traffic of Ben Hart's big boots, and Doc Easy's store shoes and the rubber-soled things the ambulance men wore — and, as far as that went. his own shoes too. But still, unmistakable, one pointy-toe going into the living room, and the same pointy-toe coming back. None of the other footprints from beneath the spare room window.

He stood up again at last. So now he thought he could reconstruct what had happened, although he still had no idea why. No matter. He had a trail to follow, and if he had to he would track a shadow through Hell and catch up with its substance on the other side.

He let himself out of the house and closed the door as best he could. Later he'd get someone up here to fix that broken lock. Right now he wanted to talk to Don Hastings, who would not be caught dead in a pair of Beatle boots, and so would seem to be without connection to this affair — but Johnny was running on instinct and emotion now, logic set aside.

7

The National Crime Information Center was located in
Washington, D. C., and when Sergeant Tony Lopez
thought about it, which was no oftener than he had to, he
pictured it as built around some kind of vast light-blinking,
reel-turning, softly humming monster effortlessly and elec-
tronically (in Tony's mind they were synonymous)
matching innumerable bits of information and spewing out
a steady flow of conclusions. The concept made him
uneasy. On the other hand, NCIC did make a great deal of
police work easier, and in some instances was all that made
it even possible.

Here, for example, was a notice that the $650 wrist
watch reported stolen from Don Hastings had turned up in
a hock shop in San Antonio, Texas, seven hundred miles
away. And the funny thing was that the man who hocked
the watch claimed that he had bought the thing, all open
and above board, in Juarez, Mexico, half the state of Texas
back to the west, and still a long day's drive from Santo
Cristo. That, of course, would have to be checked, if
possible, but the important thing was that the blinking
monster at NCIC had put it all together and then even
known what to do with the information after it had it.
Tony wondered what they would think of next.

On his desk too was Saul Pentland's formal report on

39

the .357 Magnum Colt Python belonging to Don Hastings. There was no doubt that it was the gun that had killed Miss Lucy Carruthers, and the fact that the only fingerprints on it were those of Don Hastings himself made you wonder if the gun, unlike the wrist watch, had indeed ever been stolen in the first place. Tony would have been pleased if he had known that his thoughts in this direction paralleled those of Cassie Enright. Tony had a great deal of respect for Cassie, who was not only a good-looking chick but was packed with brains and education as well. Toward Cassie and the rest of the scientific types associated with the museum, Tony felt the same kind of awe that the mysterious NCIC inspired. People, and machines, like that took two and two and then told you where to go to find the missing two to make six, or maybe even seven. That Johnny Ortiz did the same thing, but he did it or seemed to do it by some kind of magic.

The phone rang on Tony's desk. He picked it up and spoke his name. Johnny's voice, as soft and as angry as Tony had ever heard it, said, "Don Hastings. I want him. He isn't home, and he hasn't been. I'll be at the hospital." The phone went dead.

Tony hung up. He made a small bow to the wall. *"A sus órdenes,"* he said, "Ours not to question why." He got up to set wheels in motion.

Doc Easy was in surgery. Johnny walked over to the snack bar and had a cup of not-very-good coffee while he waited. In hospitals, he thought, as in bus stations, railroad stations, and these days even in airports, you found all kinds of people with only one thing in common: each was wrapped up in his own little world — and why should that kind of damn-fool idea pop into his mind at a time like this?

Behind him a man's voice said in rapid, slurred Spanish, *"Mamacita,* he will be all right. I tell you. The doctor has sworn it."

And a woman's voice, almost whispering, said, *Santa María, Madre de Dios, por favor, por favor!"*

Johnny put down his paper cup and walked away. He wondered what it would be like to be able to pray, and mean it – and to whom? He sought and found some of that store of inherited patience and withdrew into his shell. Sooner or later, he told himself, all waiting came to an end.

It was well over an hour before they called him to the desk to say that Doc Easy was back in his office and could see him now. (*Walk, don't run, to the nearest exit* . . . Johnny knocked and walked in.)

Doc wore still his surgical pajamas and that silly little Nehru cap. He was smoking a cigarette, inhaling deeply, making himself relax. "I think she'll be all right," he said. "She took a beating, but she's young and healthy, strong." He stopped and studied Johnny's face. "Do you know who did it?"

"Not quite. Not yet."

"Do you know why it was done?"

Johnny took a deep breath. "Was she raped?"

"No."

"Then," Johnny said, "I don't know why." He sat there, immobile, expressionless, fighting for control over the sense of frustration. "There were three of them," he said presently, "probably kids, from the shoes they wore."

Doc's eyebrows rose. "You can tell?"

"I can tell," Johnny said, and let it go at that. "One of them, and only one, went into the living room. He switched on the lamp and then went around smashing things. Finally he smashed the lamp too and went back to

41

the bedroom." After, or during the time Cassie was being beaten? Did it matter? Johnny sat silent.

"Robbery?" Doc said. "There's been a lot of it in the papers."

"I don't think anything was taken, any more than it was at the Carruthers house." Johnny stood up then. *"Basta,"* he said. Can I see her?"

"She is under heavy sedation."

"It doesn't matter. Maybe somehow she'll know I'm there."

Maybe. It was impossible to tell. He stood at the bedside and touched Cassie's hand, brushed her cheek gently with his fingertips. *"Chica."* It was almost a whisper. "Just take it easy. It's going to be all right." Talking to himself? Maybe. He could see no response, and after a few moments he left the room, walked down the hallway and on through the main lobby, outside at last into the bright sun.

As he walked to his car he glanced up at the nearby mountains. They were sharp against the sky, unmoving, unmoved, unaffected by lives or by people. On their upper slopes snow still lay plain; beneath, the cool green of aspen covered the harshness and the rock. High above the great peaks a jet transport drew a contrail like a moving white pencil mark on a blue slate.

Word spread as it always did in Santo Cristo. Cassie's hospital room began to fill with flowers; and as the heavy sedation wore away and her eyes came again into focus, she stared at the flowers and took comfort from the thought that lay behind them, while she tried without success to remember what had happened, and why — most particularly why.

Her head was one large throbbing ache and there was

a constriction, which she properly identified as tape, binding at least four of her ribs. She kept her breathing shallow, because deep breaths hurt way down inside where she had never experienced pain before; and this was frightening, but there was nothing to do but bear with it. That first day she did little but endure.

In the evening old Ben Hart came to see her wearing a voluminous oilskin riding poncho, although, as nearly as Cassie could tell, there was no sign of rain in the world outside. The poncho was explained when Chico emerged from its depths, writhing in ecstasy, one foreleg splinted and bound. He licked Cassie's hand and thumped the bedclothes with his tail and made small whimpering sounds of joy. "He's quite a character," Ben said. "Shouldn't wonder if he grows up into a good-sized beast. Hope so. How you doing, honey?" Pause. "Don't answer that. Silly damn question. Anything you need?"

Will Carston was the next visitor. "Sid Thomas sends his best," Will said, "but he will not even go near a hospital if he can help it." Sid was Will's contemporary, an artist who in 1920 with half of one lung gone, and the remaining lung-and-a-half tainted by mustard gas, had come west to Santo Cristo to die. Now, fifty years later, with no more than half of one lung left, Sid figured it had been a good bargain.

The last visitor that evening was Johnny. He came in slowly, almost hesitantly, and his eyes studied Cassie's. What he found there seemed to relax him, and some of the harshness went out of his face. He bent over the bed and his lips brushed Cassie's cheek. *"Chica —"* He had no more words. He shook his head helplessly.

"I lied to you," Cassie said, "but you knew that already, didn't you? I'm sorry." She felt no pain in the saying.

"It doesn't matter."

Cassie waggled her head faintly on the pillow. Some of the evening remained clear in her mind, and she drew on the memory. "Don was in El Rincón with a girl — but you found that out too, didn't you?"

Johnny's eyebrows rose. "The point is," he said, "how did you know?"

"I asked down Arroyo Road, just as you did." Something tugged at her mind and was gone. Maybe when the throbbing aches diminished the something would return. Maybe.

"Chica." Johnny's voice was solemn. "Leave it to us, me. You go around asking questions —"

There it was: the something reappearing in her mind without warning. "That's what he said — Billy Joe Harmon."

Johnny watched her in silence.

"I ran into him by accident. He went into bars with me and then walked me home. He said that if you, the police, were interested, then I'd do well to stay out of it."

"He was right, whoever he is." Johnny tucked the name Billy Joe Harmon away in his mind. And now for the big question. "Can you remember anything about what happened, *chica?"*

"I'm sorry. I've tried."

"There were three of them," Johnny said. "Does that help at all?"

It was obvious the number meant nothing. "I'm sorry, Johnny."

"They came in through your study window. You were in bed." He watched her shiver faintly, and he was tempted to stop the questioning, but he had to try. "Nothing is missing that I can see," Johnny said, "so I don't think they came to steal." Her eyes watched him

44

soberly. "And they didn't have rape in mind." Her eyes closed briefly. She made no move, no sound. Johnny said gently, "Nothing comes back?"

"I'm sorry, Johnny."

He nodded then. "Never mind, *chica*. We'll find them."

For a long time she was silent. Then, "You're a hunter, Johnny."

Johnny nodded again. "It's my job."

Tony Lopez had gone home, but he had left a message for Johnny at headquarters. "Hastings hasn't been seen since yesterday afternoon. His car is gone, but he hasn't drawn any cash out of the bank and he hasn't touched at the airports, so it's probably that he hasn't gone far. The night boys will keep an eye on the house, and if he turns up they'll let you know."

Suspicious behavior? Maybe; maybe not. The man might just have gone off on a fling with the Anglo chick with the Texas accent. Johnny put the message aside.

There was a Billy Joe Harmon listed in the telephone directory — not William Joseph; Billy Joe. Johnny called the number. There was no answer. No matter. It could wait until tomorrow. Today had been a long day.

He went home and went to bed. His last thought was of Cassie and the way she had looked at him when he walked into the hospital room.

8

There was a burglary that night at the home of Waldo and
Dotty Marks. Waldo had retired as a major appliance dealer
in Corpus Christi, Texas, shrewdly putting the franchises in
the hands of his son-in-law, and he and Dotty had come to
higher and cooler Santo Cristo to enjoy life. They had
built a splendid house with a view of the mountains, and
they had established, with local Spanish labor, a garden to
match Lucy Carruthers' own. Both Waldo and Dotty
belonged to the Santo Cristo Garden Club. There was a
meeting that night. The burglary took place while Waldo
and Dotty were attending the meeting.

Sergeant Tony Lopez took down the data the next
morning at headquarters. At the beginning it went
smoothly enough.

"Dotty's — my wife's jewelry," Waldo said. "We have
an inventory, of course, and that's being checked right
now. We'll be able to give you a complete list." He was an
apple-cheeked little man with a salesman's confident
approach. "Trinkets, too," he said, "some of them valu-
able. And then the silverware. We've collected that silverware for forty years, and we didn't start with one of the
stock patterns in the first place, no, sir. It was an English
pattern, handmade, and all the pieces we've added have
been handmade, too. My wife is sick about it."

Tony said he could see how that would be. The

46

silverware had been in a mahogany chest, and it, too, was inventoried. "A list of all the pieces of a special pattern," Tony said. "It may make our work quite a bit easier, Mr. Marks." He thought of the humming monster at the National Crime Information Center.

"I doubt it," Waldo said. He had his opinions and he was used to having them listened to. "The way this country is today, nobody willing to work, kids with too much money and too little respect for anybody or anything." His voice was dry and bitter. "These Mex kids here in Santo Cristo —"

"We call them Spanish-Americans," Tony said.

"What's the difference? They'll steal you blind or knife you if they can get you in 'a dark alley — long hair, tight pants, those pointed-toe boots, *pachucos* every one of them and I wish they'd go back where they came from."

Privately, Tony's opinion of some of the Santo Cristo youth was identical with Waldo's, but he would not for the world have admitted it. After all, he was Spanish-American too. "The ancestors of most of them, Mr. Marks," he said, "were living here before the first Anglo even thought of moving to this part of the world." He almost, but not quite, added, "Maybe the Anglos ought to go back where *they* came from." Instead he stood up and said politely, "I'll be in touch, Mr. Marks."

Waldo had the funny feeling that he had somehow been put down, and he liked it not. On the other hand, even though he stood on tippy-toe, the top of his head came only about to Tony Lopez's chin, and things you might say to a man on your own level were best forgotten when you had to shout them up that far. Even to a Mex. "I should hope so," Waldo said, and strutted to the doorway.

Tony suddenly remembered something Johnny Ortiz

47

had said. "The Garden Club meeting," he said.

Waldo stopped, turned. "What about it?"

"Would anyone have known that you and Mrs. Marks were going to it?"

"We never miss a meeting. Not in four years." It was obvious that Waldo resented any implication of inconstancy.

"That wasn't exactly what I meant, Mr. Marks. Would anyone have known that there was a meeting last night, at what time it would be held, and that you and Mrs. Marks were going to it?"

"The meetings," Waldo said stiffly, "are always mentioned in the newspaper, on the society page. And afterwards there is always another mention, listing the members who attended. The Garden Club, sergeant —" He stopped. His apple cheeks contracted and Waldo's eyes took on a shrewdness he rarely allowed to be seen. "I see what you mean," he said. "Somebody plans these things by reading the newspapers, knowing when folks aren't going to be home?"

"Possible," Tony said.

"That doesn't sound like snot-nosed Mex kids."

No, it did not, Tony thought; and wondered what the softly humming monster at NCIC could make of that. Probably nothing; the monster ingested facts, not hypotheses. Tony wished he were in the same lucky situation. "Thank you, Mr. Marks," he said.

Billy Joe Harmon was with a potential customer in the automobile showroom. Johnny stood by and listened idly. "A real fine automobile," Billy Joe was saying, "or motor car, as our British friends might say. Real fine. Why don't you take a little drive, sir, and find out for yourself just how she handles? We have one outside, and the key is in it, and I would be mighty pleased if you would give it a try. Try them all, I always say, and *then* decide." He was still talking as he led the potential customer away. He was back in a few minutes. "Now, sir," he said to Johnny, "what can I do for you?" His eyes appeared to be measuring and appraising: a new car? used? compact? full-size model? maybe a pick-up truck? or a camper? "Billy Joe Harmon, sir," he added. "At your service."

Johnny showed his badge and watched Billy Joe's face for reaction. There was none, except, perhaps, mild disappointment. "A couple of questions," Johnny said. "You were with Dr. Cassandra Enright night before last on Canyon Road." Now why did he feel that he had to use Cassie's full name and title?

"I had that honor, sir."

"Bar-hopping," Johnny said.

Billy Joe looked as if he was about to make something of that statement, and then thought better of it. "We were making inquiries," he said, "concerning the recent whereabouts of a certain person."

He was behaving now, Johnny thought, like a road-show *southron gemmun* of the old school who felt that his *honnuh* had been impugned. Balls. "Don Hastings," Johnny said. "I know all about it. Then you walked Cassie home, is that right?"

"That is correct, sir, absolutely correct." Senator Claghorn now.

"You warned her that if the police were interested in Don Hastings, she'd better stay out of it. What made you think that?"

"I should think," Billy Joe said slowly, "that what happened to Dr. Enright shows I wasn't just shying at moonbeams, lieutenant. In my business you meet all kinds, you do indeed, and if there's one thing I've learned from

49

Fort Worth to Waco to El Paso to Santo Cristo, it is that when the *po*lice are interested, honest folks had better stay out of the way. I am shocked by what happened to Dr. Enright, and I hope and pray that you will bring the rascals responsible to justice."

Johnny thought about it. "You think, then," he said, "that what happened to Cassie was a warning to stop asking questions?"

"I didn't say that, sir. Like the late Will Rogers, all I know is what I read in the newspapers. And what I listen to talked about here and yon." Another pause. "But they didn't steal anything, and they didn't *mo*lest the lady sexually, the way I hear it, so maybe some kind of warning was exactly what they had in mind, wouldn't you say, lieutenant?"

"Possible," Johnny said. More than possible: probable; he had been thinking the same. "Thanks, Mr. Harmon."

"Billy Joe." The outraged *southron gemmun* was gone, and Senator Claghorn; the salesman had returned. The man had an actor's talent for throwing himself into a role; an actor's, or a circuit-riding Bible-banger's. "Everybody calls me Billy Joe. When folks call me Mr. Harmon, I always think they're talking to my daddy."

Back at headquarters Tony Lopez followed Johnny into his office. In a way, Tony thought, what he had to say was funny, in another way it was maddening. Those goddam Anglos and their irresponsible behavior. "Don Hastings," Tony said. "We've found him."

Johnny leaned against the corner of his desk. He said nothing, and his eyes, angry eyes, watched Tony's face.

"Just happened to run across him," Tony said. "Fellow I know saw him. You know where? Up the Pecos.

50

He's fishing. Had a couple of nice rainbow, this fellow said." He stopped there to await Johnny's reaction.

"Hijo de puta!" Johnny said softly, with feeling.

Tony nodded. "I felt more or less the same. I didn't know he had a cabin up there, did you? And he has a chick with him."

"Oh?" Johnny was interested now. The chick with the Texas accent? The one who was with Hastings the night Miss Lucy was shot? "Do you know where the cabin is?"

Tony did. He produced a sketch map and gave it to Johnny. "And," Tony said, "you got a visitor. Fellow named Carruthers, Lowell Carruthers, straight from Boston, wants to know what's being done about Miss Lucy's murder. You want to see him?"

Lowell Carruthers wore a dark-gray, summer suit, black loafers, a white button-down shirt, and a neat bow tie. He was a small man, with white hair cut short. His age could have been anywhere between sixty and seventy-five. Polite, but not to be trifled with; that much was evident. "Lucy Carruthers was my first cousin," he said. His voice was a faintly nasal tenor. "I am her closest relation."

"Don Hastings?" Johnny said.

"Donald, of course," Carruthers said. "Lucy was his aunt. Donald's father —" He stopped. "No matter, lieutenant. You are not interested in our family skeletons."

"I might be."

Carruthers thought about it. Presently he nodded. "I see your point. If and when that particular family skeleton becomes germane to your investigation, I shall see that you have all the facts." Pause. "Do you know where Donald is, by the way? He is not at home."

"He's gone fishing."

The corners of Carruthers' eyes wrinkled in amusement. He nodded. "In character, lieutenant. Donald's motto, inherited from his father, has always been: if there is unpleasantness, run, do not walk, to the nearest exit."

It was obviously not Lowell Carruthers' motto. In his way, which was not Johnny's way, the two separated by thousands of miles and generations of different cultures, Lowell Carruthers was a tough little man. "I'm going up to see Hastings," Johnny said. "Do you want to come along?"

There was no hesitation. "Thank you, lieutenant. I do indeed."

They took Johnny's pick-up. There was a deer rifle in the rack mounted across the rear window. Carruthers did not miss it. Johnny smiled. "More or less standard equipment," he said, "like the shovel in back and the tow cable and the water bag. From time to time they all come in handy."

"In films and on television," Carruthers said, "men out here wear side arms."

"And the damndest thing is," Johnny said, "when they shoot, they hit what they're shooting at, too."

There was a short silence. Then, "I see," Carruthers said.

"Hand guns," Johnny said, "are good for killing people at very close range." He glanced at Carruthers' face. "Old ladies sometimes."

Carruthers digested the statement without expression. "That was how Lucy was killed? The weapon has been established?"

"One of Hastings' hand guns. Which he had reported stolen. But the next morning it was there in his gun cabinet." Stated baldly like that, Johnny thought, it sounded very damning indeed. He wondered what Carruthers would think.

52

Carruthers said slowly, "Unless Donald has changed a great deal, lieutenant, I cannot see him pulling a trigger at anything animate, let alone a human being who has always terrified him." Pause. "Did you know Cousin Lucy?" Rhetorical question; he waited for no answer. "One of our ancestors marched to Quebec with Arnold. Another commanded a clipper ship and is credited with putting down a mutiny single-handed, with only a belaying pin and his bare fists." He watched Johnny grin. "Others of our family were not above indulging in the slave trade. You begin to see the picture I am trying to sketch? Cousin Lucy was born out of her time. She was a throwback to those earlier, more violent days. She had the lovable disposition of a snapping turtle, and if Donald ever worked up the courage even to face her with a gun in his hand, I have lived a long life and learned nothing." He paused again. "I have an idea," he said, "that something of the same thinking has been in your mind. Otherwise, I cannot see why Donald is fishing instead of sitting in a jail cell."

There was nothing wrong with Lowell Carruthers' perception, either, Johnny thought. He grinned. "Something like that," he said.

They left the divided highway on a two-lane road that wound through piñon, juniper, and bare rock. Around them mountains crowded the sky. "I know nothing of this country," Carruthers said. "When Lucy spoke of it she tended to babble with such enthusiasm that there was no separating fact from fiction. Some of the dates she mentioned." He shook his head.

"Coronado came through this pass," Johnny said, "in 1541. He went as far as what is now Kansas, didn't find what he was looking for, killed a couple of guides who had lied to him, and came on back." Sometimes you tended to forget that this was a land with a long violent history. Johnny thought of Cassie lying in her hospital bed.

53

Because she had asked questions about Don Hastings? How did that make sense?

Carruthers said, "Eighty years more or less before the Pilgrims landed at Plymouth. Were your ancestors here then, lieutenant?"

"Some of them. A little farther south." Johnny was probably about to astonish Carruthers, whose ancestry was no doubt homogeneous; and the thought amused him. "The Indian ancestors, that is. I don't know who the Anglo or the Spanish ancestors were." A few months ago would he have been able to say that with ease? Before Cassie? He turned to smile at Carruthers. "My mother was an Apache," he said. "She lived all her life on the reservation."

The corners of Carruthers' eyes crinkled again. "And do you go about scalping people, lieutenant?"

Smiling still, "Not often," Johnny said. He was not even faintly tempted to break into the Leo Carillo Spanish-American accent. Strange.

9

The road climbed out of the piñon-juniper belt into a forest of ponderosa pine with here and there scattered firs and spruce. They had come to the river, clear and turbulent, and the road followed its winding course. "Aspen," Johnny said. He pointed to the pale chartreuse trunks startling amongst the evergreens. "That means we're at eight thousand feet."

"I am impressed, lieutenant."

"Hastings' cabin is just a little farther on." Pause. Then, with a delicacy Johnny had not known he possessed, "Hastings isn't alone. According to reports, he has a girl with him." He glanced at Carruthers' face.

"Even in Boston, lieutenant," Carruthers said, "we are acquainted with the birds and the bees." For a third time the corners of his eyes crinkled. "Despite what you may have heard, we do not consider breeding everything, but we do find it pleasurable. Donald's father was quite fond of females, too."

The cabin was set back in the trees and protected by a stout fence and gate. Johnny opened the gate, drove through, and got out to close the gate carefully after them. They drove up a rutted track and parked behind a large station wagon. Hastings walked out on the porch of the cabin and watched Johnny step down from the pick-up.

His attitude seemed to be watchful, neither truculent nor apprehensive; but he did show surprise when Carruthers appeared, and Johnny, watching Hastings' face, decided that respect, even deference, was what he found in it.

A girl walked out of the cabin and stood beside Hastings. She was a large girl, barefoot, wearing hip-rider jeans and a tank top and, obviously, no brassiere; when she walked, her large high breasts jounced and the nipples showed plain crowding the thin fabric. There was no mistaking her attitude: it was defiant. "Some people just drop in, without warning, don't they, honey?" she said. Texas accent.

Hastings said politely, "Cousin Lowell."

"Donald," Carruthers said. "The lieutenant was kind enough to bring me along."

"Oh, good God!" the girl said, "fuzz? *And* the blue-blood family establishment representative? Too much."

"Does the young woman have a name, Donald?" Carruthers' voice was mild, polite.

"Tess baby," Hastings said, "why don't you go inside? They want to talk to me."

"To both of you," Johnny said. In the silence he and Carruthers walked up on the porch.

Hastings took a deep breath. "Is there some kind of law that says I can't come up here to my own cabin and go fishing?" Bravado, but hollow; the harmonics were false.

"Not that I know of," Johnny said.

"Then what are you fixing to bust us for, fuzz?" This was Tess baby.

"That depends," Johnny said. "Three nights ago, when Lucy Carruthers was shot, you two had a drink in El Rincón. Then where did you go?" He was guessing, of course, but it almost had to be the same girl.

"That," the girl said, "is none of your damn business."

Johnny looked at Hastings and waited. Hastings said, "I don't see that I have to answer anything."

"True," Johnny said. "You don't. Your aunt was shot with your gun, which you had reported stolen, but which was in your gun cabinet the next morning." He shrugged. "But you don't have to answer anything, here, or in jail. That's your privilege."

"Now, wait a minute," Hastings said.

Carruthers said, "Don't be any more of a damned fool than you have always been, Donald." His tone was both sharp and weary, as if he had met this situation before and his patience had long since worn thin.

Hastings looked at the girl. She shrugged. "So tell them. Who cares?"

Hastings said, "We went to Tess's place."

Tess shook her head. "If you're going to tell it, honey, tell it straight. It isn't my pad. I was just staying there for a night or two." She was looking straight at Johnny. "It belongs to a chick named Sue Bright. You know her?"

Johnny nodded without expression. "She's a friend of yours?"

"Not particularly. I met her in a bar and went home with her. Do you want to make something of that?"

"Vice and morals aren't in my line," Johnny said. He looked at Hastings again. "So you went there from El Rincón?"

"That's what I said." Hastings was trying hard to ignore Cousin Lowell's presence; it was uphill work. The ferocious mustache seemed merely pitiful now, pure masquerade.

"How long were you there?" Johnny said.

Hastings hesitated. "All night."

"Just the two of you?"

Tess said suddenly, explosively, "For God's sake,

fuzz, do you want a diagram? Sue was there. There were three of us. Do you get it now?"

Carruthers said, "I think the point is reasonably clear."

"Are you shocked, dad?"

Carruthers looked at the girl for a long time in silence. Then, slowly, he shook his head. "Your generation hasn't invented anything new, young woman," he said. "I don't think you have even enlarged on the old." He looked again at Hastings. "And you haven't changed either, have you, Donald?"

Johnny said, "Night before last, where were you?"

"Here." Hastings' voice was sulky.

Johnny nodded. He looked at Carruthers. "That's all I wanted. You?"

"I have had a great sufficiency," Carruthers said. He turned away and walked down the porch steps. Johnny followed him. They got into the pick-up. As they drove away, Johnny looked back in the side mirror. Hastings was still standing on the porch ignoring the girl who was tugging at his arm.

They drove in silence for a time. Carruthers said at last, "Do you believe his — alibi?"

"Maybe. Sue Bright would say anything."

Carruthers said, "There is still the matter of Donald's character. He is, he has always been, weak."

"Only one thing," Johnny said. "The bartender at El Rincón says he was stoned, probably on both alcohol and marihuana. And the bartender also says that when Hastings is stoned he can turn mean."

Carruthers sighed. "I see," he said, and that was all.

Johnny dropped Carruthers at the Inn. "I thank you for the ride, lieutenant, and the talk. I appreciate your frankness."

58

"De nada." Johnny hesitated. "I'll be in touch." He smiled suddenly. "I may want to know about those family skeletons."

Carruthers smiled and nodded as he turned away. Johnny drove off.

Next stop Sue Bright's studio. Sue was home. She was a slim woman customarily, as now, in blue jeans and sneakers, shirt sleeves rolled up on her tanned arms. She was a photographer of more than regional reputation, specializing in conservation subjects, with portraiture as a paying sideline. She was in her middle thirties, independent, and frank to the point of bluntness. "Tess?" she said. She nodded. "She posed for me. She's a rotten model, doesn't know how to handle herself, but she has a lovely body."

"Three nights ago," Johnny said, "that was Tuesday, she spent the night here?"

"What if she did?"

"I'm asking," Johnny said.

"And you expect to be answered." Sue smiled faintly. "Why not? Tess spent Tuesday night here."

"Was there anybody else?"

"Nosy, aren't you? Who's your candidate?"

"I'm still asking."

Sue hesitated. Then she shrugged. "Don Hastings was here too. He came in with Tess. Make of that whatever you want."

"What time did they come in?"

"Eight, eight-thirty, I don't watch the clock."

"Hastings spent the whole night here too?"

"Does it matter?"

"If it didn't," Johnny said, "I wouldn't be asking. And I don't give a damn about your morals."

"Touchy, aren't we?" Sue was smiling broadly now.

"You see, I don't give a damn whether you give a damn or not. I live my life the way I want to live it, and how I live it is nobody's business but mine." The smile was suddenly gone. "For the record, yes, Don baby spent the night here. Along about midnight he passed out. He snores."

It rang true enough, Johnny thought. On the other hand, Sue Bright could probably lie with a straight face if she wanted to; it was Johnny's experience that most females like Sue Bright could. But why should she? Good question. "Had Tess known Hastings before Tuesday night?" he said.

"I doubt it. Tess is a very friendly girl. I gather she just bumped into him on Arroyo Road, had a drink with him, and brought him here for the fun of it." Sue paused. "He wasn't much fun. He never is when he's stoned." She paused again. "Anything else? I have some darkroom work to do."

"Nothing more now," Johnny said. "Thanks." He started for the door. Sue's voice stopped him.

"You might be interested in these," she said, and held out a batch of large matte photographs.

Johnny shuffled through them. They were all of Tess, nude. When he looked up, Sue was smiling at him again. "You do nice work," Johnny said and tossed the photographs on the table as he walked out.

He drove to the hospital and walked down the long silent corridor to Cassie's room. Her door was open, and even in the corridor the scent of flowers was plain. Hell, Johnny thought; why do I always remember things like flowers too late? No answer. He knocked and walked in.

Cassie was sitting up in bed. Her hair was combed and the almost translucent look had disappeared from her lips and eyelids; her nostrils were no longer pinched with pain. She could smile. "I hoped you would come."

"You knew I'd come, *chica.*" He bent over the bed to kiss her gently. Then he sat down in the visitor's chair. "For openers," he said, "I saw your Billy Joe Harmon. How did you get mixed up with that character?"

Cassie told him about the boys' club and Billy Joe's request that she give her slide lecture to the boys. "He said they needed a sense of pride in their origins, and maybe he's right."

Johnny thought of Lowell Carruthers and his pride of ancestry. "Maybe." He smiled. "Maybe we're the lucky ones, *chica,* you and I." He was not precisely sure what he meant, except that a Don Hastings, with the same background as Lowell Carruthers, all the advantages of wealth and breeding, had goofed off into what he was now, and it seemed to Johnny that it must have taken quite a bit of doing considering what he started from. "I'm no sociologist," he said, "thank God." He paused. "Do you know Sue Bright?"

Cassie's smile spread. "What are you doing with her?"

"The girl with Don Hastings Tuesday night is a girl named Tess, probably run away from the family oil wells. She apparently picked him up and took him to Sue's studio, where she'd been staying. Tess and Sue are his alibi for that night." He paused. "Do you believe it, *chica?*" Cassie's lie about being with Don Hastings herself Tuesday night was forgotten; forgotten, or now and forever ignored.

Cassie said, "What is Tess like?"

Johnny described her. He summed it up. "Wild, far out, probably open to anything for kicks."

Cassie nodded slowly. "Could be."

"Then," Johnny said, "how does what happened to you make any sense?"

Cassie closed her eyes. "I've been trying to remember." She shook her head faintly, and opened her eyes again. "Nothing. I'm sorry, Johnny."

"Don't worry about it." He made himself smile. "Visitors?"

Cassie smiled and nodded. "Ben Hart with Chico. Carlos. Will Carston. Flora Hobbs. Billy Joe Harmon." Her smile spread. "Jealous?"

His smile matched hers. "I'll let you know."

10

"A couple of things," Johnny said, "and I think we'd better run them down." He leaned against the corner of Tony Lopez's desk. "First, where was Miss Lucy Carruthers going that night when she found she was out of gas?"

"Quién sabe?" Tony said, and added, "What difference?"

"I want to know," Johnny said, and was not quite sure why. "Was there a meeting of some kind, or a gallery opening? Was there a party? And when she didn't show, why wasn't she missed? Did she keep an engagement book? What does it say about that night?"

Tony sighed. "Okay. I have the message."

"And," Johnny said, "I want to know what Hastings was doing the night his place was burglarized."

"You could ask him."

Johnny shook his head. "I don't want to have to guess whether he's lying. Maybe he was bar-hopping. Alone? That wouldn't make much sense. He could have gone home any time. But if he was with somebody?" He was silent for a few moments, thoughtful.

"Oh, God," Tony said, "what now?"

"The night Miss Lucy was killed," Johnny said. *"If* Hastings is telling the truth, and the Magnum actually was stolen, then it had to be returned that night after it shot her, no?"

Tony merely nodded. Johnny didn't usually labor the obvious, but Tony didn't see what he was driving at this time.

"And Hastings was with Tess and went to Sue Bright's with her and spent the night. Coincidence? Or plan? Did Tess pick him up to keep him out of the way so the gun could be returned?" He paused. "No, the timing is wrong. He was already with Tess when the gun was fired." Another pause. "Still, whoever returned the gun was taking an awful chance unless he knew that Hastings wasn't home and wouldn't be coming home."

"If the gun was ever stolen in the first place," Tony said, "and I like it better if it wasn't."

"And Tess, Sue Bright, and Hastings are all lying about where Hastings spent the night?" Johnny stood away from the desk. "Possible," he said. "I wouldn't trust any one of them around the corner." He started for the doorway, and then stopped. "Fellow named Billy Joe Harmon," he said, "automobile salesman, has set up a kind of club for Spanish kids — you know anything about it?"

Tony nodded. "That shed back of Montoya's yard. At least it keeps some of the kids out of the plaza."

That afternoon was cloudless, the high, dry air a tonic — a Santo Cristo day. *Turistas* strolled the plaza. Behind the town high above the foothills a single rough-legged hawk soared endlessly, riding the thermals without effort. South of town, a turkey vulture circled, his flight less steady, but his circling more purposeful, than that of the hawk. A second vulture joined the circling, and a third . . .

The two boys, Anglos, riding motor bikes, skidded into the gas station as if the Devil himself were after them. Pepe Martinez watched his gravel scatter and swore to himself with feeling. The damn kids probably wouldn't buy a gallon of gas between them, Pepe thought. He was almost willing to bet that all they wanted was free air from his hose; or maybe the use of his telephone.

The telephone guess was close to right, although neither boy wanted to make the call himself. "You do it," one of the boys said. "I tell you, he's dead! Shot! Lying there with the whole front of his shirt bloody and his eyes wide open!"

"Madre de Dios!" Pepe said, and then hesitated, natural caution taking over. "Are you putting me on?"

"I promise! He's there!"

The second boy swallowed painfully. His eyes were on the sky. "If you won't believe us," he said, "look!" He pointed upward. There were five vultures now, swinging lower in tight circles over the nearby hills.

"Madre de Dios!" Pepe said again, and this time went to the phone.

At headquarters the desk man listened, then switched the call to Tony Lopez. Pepe Martinez's voice was unsteady. "The two boys, they say there is a man dead. And there are buzzards. They say the man have been shot."

"Okay," Tony said. Then, in rapid Spanish, "Keep the boys there. You understand? We will arrive immediately."

"Understood." Martinez's voice was happier in Spanish.

Johnny drove his pick-up. Tony Lopez rode with him. The two boys were waiting on their trail bikes. They blasted out onto the highway into the lead position with a further scattering of Pepe Martinez's gravel. Ahead, lower now, seven vultures circled warily. "The upper end of the Arroyo Hondo," Tony said. He sighed. "Looks like we walk."

A dirt road left the highway and wound back into the

foothills. They followed it for a time, and then the boys turned off the dirt road on a narrow rutted track, and the pick-up stayed with them until the track itself became merely a trail.

Johnny stopped then, got out and beckoned the boys. "Leave the bikes here." He saw the disappointment in their faces. "If the buzzards know what they're doing," he said, "it isn't far. And I don't want you riding all over any tracks there may be." He started up the trail without waiting for a reply. The bike engines died reluctantly. The sudden quiet was relief.

It was a plain and well-used trail. There were beer cans, and empty cigarette packages, here and there a discharged shotgun shell, an empty flattened .22 cartridge box, the usual litter scattered in the chamisa and grama grass. Three piñon jays rose screaming in protest at the human invasion. A cottontail rabbit abandoned immobility for dodging flight. A small skink scuttled into the safety of a dry Russian thistle. The vultures continued their circling, but at a safer altitude.

Johnny walked steadily, his eyes sweeping the trail, seeing the tracks of the bikes, and footprints, some faint, some clear. Here a recent coyote dropping indicated that the cottontail rabbit had better watch his step. There a pug mark spelled bobcat. There were deer tracks in profusion; probably the deer laid up by day in the higher ground, and came down at night to the trickle of water in the bottom of the arroyo. It passed through Johnny's mind what Cassie had said about his being a hunter. Well, it was true, but most times, as now, he hunted man, not animals. And there the man was.

He was only a boy, sixteen, seventeen, hard to tell the exact age. Spanish-American, dark skin, glossy black over-long hair, sideburns, tight black trousers, Beatle boots, a fancy frilled white shirt, its front stained hideously red now. He lay partly on his back, one leg tucked up in an odd, strained position, his arms a little out from his sides. His eyes were open, and already filmed with dust. There was no mistake: he was dead.

The two boys, their sense of shock wearing off now, started to move closer. "Stay where you are," Johnny said without looking up. He moved slowly in a circle around the body, studying the ground. Then he hunkered down and spoke over his shoulder. "Tony." And when Tony's shadow appeared, still without looking up, Johnny pointed. "There and there and there. His footprints, plain."

Tony said, "So?"

Johnny looked up then. "I've seen them before. Twice. Once at Miss Lucy Carruthers', and once in Cassie Enright's house." Silence.

Johnny stood up and looked around, distantly this time. He pointed to an outcropping of pink lichen-covered rock a hundred yards away. "That's the likely spot. He was standing facing the way I am. He was shot in front. No blood on the ground. I think we'll find the bullet still in him — if there's anything left of it."

"There usually is," Tony said.

"I could be wrong," Johnny said, "but I'm thinking of one of those overpowered .22's, around four-thousand-feet-per-second muzzle velocity. If that's it, all we'll find will be fragments." He looked once more at the body.

Just a kid, he thought: *drop out, turn on* — but maybe *drop out* not from free choice, but because it was an Anglo world and unless you had a thorough command of the basic tool of that world, the English language, then schooling became more and more incomprehensible until at last it was unbearable; and *turn on,* not with drugs as the middle-class Anglo kids did, but with rage and resentment. What difference how, or why? The kid was dead. Still, the wonderment remained. "Back to the pick-up," he said to Tony. "Call in and tell them what we need – Doc Easy, some photographs, ambulance to take him in. I'm going to look at those rocks." He watched Tony start off. "Oh," Johnny said, "and take these boys with you. Get their names. We'll want to thank them. Maybe a picture in the paper."

11

Cassie was sitting in a chair in her hospital room when Johnny came in that night. "Like a big girl," Johnny said, and bent to kiss her gently. He took the visitor's chair, stretched out his legs and sighed. "We've got a new one, *chica.*"

"I heard on the radio. Have you identified him yet?" She tried to keep all emotion out of her voice – as an anthropologist should, she told herself; and found a world of difference between thinking about the here and now, the recently dead, and those who had lived, and disappeared, hundreds of years ago. "Why, Johnny?" Pause. "Do you know?"

"Just guesswork, too much guesswork. He was at your house that night." He watched her eyes close and then open again, and he smiled at her in sympathy. "And he was at Lucy Carruthers' house sometime during the day she was shot."

"His footprints?" She had watched the tracker at work, and although a part of her mind still disbelieved, she had also seen that what he saw was real, and his reconstructions in their way as logical and precise and imaginative as those of her own discipline, which drew pictures of ways of life long since disappeared from the face of the earth.

Johnny nodded. "He was there, but what he was doing – *quién sabe?"* He shrugged. On the table beside the bed the telephone rang. Johnny said, "Maybe for me, *chica,"* and went to answer it.

Cassie watched him, smiling, thinking of his singleness of purpose and his disregard for consequences: the telephone might be for him, so he answered it ignoring the possibility that it might also be a personal call for Cassie. But I don't mind, Cassie thought; and found a sense of wonderment that it was so.

Johnny listened, nodded, said, "Thanks, Saul," and hung up. He went back to his chair. "He had fired a gun recently," he said. "Saul Pentland did a paraffin skin test on his right hand." Smiling now, he shook his head. "Just one more little fact, *chica,* like one of your shards. Maybe eventually we'll fit it in."

Cassie said, "He was at Lucy Carruthers' house that day, or night. He fired a gun recently." She too shook her head, chiding herself. "I'm trying to add one and one and make five. What else do you know about him?"

"He walked up the trail," Johnny said, "and got himself shot with a high-powered .22. There isn't enough left of the bullet to make any kind of positive identification of the rifle." He had been right in his guess of weapon. He had also been right in his estimate that the shot had come from the outcropping of pink, lichen-covered rock; the rock showed no footprints, but it was the only nearby area with a completely clear field of fire; and tiny bits of lichen had been torn away in places to suggest to Johnny's eye that a man had indeed lain there in a prone rifleman's position – a tall man; one more small fact to be fitted in. "But why he went there –" Johnny shrugged.

Cassie studied his face. "You're thinking what?"

With anyone else he would have said nothing. With

70

her he could relax and sketch his mental pictures. "He didn't walk," Johnny said, "he strutted. A city boy in shoes that were too tight. So he wouldn't just have been out for a stroll in the country."

Cassie nodded. She was smiling faintly. "Go on. He went there for a reason. To meet someone?"

"Probably. Maybe the fellow who was waiting for him with the rifle." Johnny paused. "How did he get that far out of town? If he drove, what happened to his car? He wouldn't have walked six miles. Not in those shoes. Somebody drove him."

"Or he hitchhiked," Cassie said.

Johnny thought about it. "Good girl, *chica*. Somebody on his way to Texas gave a kid a lift. Or a rancher with a pick-up. Somebody anonymous now and always." He nodded. Logical, and of course, disappointing thought, but there were always more disappointments than successes; always more game tracks than game; he had grown up with that knowledge.

Cassie said, "How about the man with the rifle?"

Another disappointment. "That outcropping," Johnny said, "runs all the way down to the highway. Somebody stayed on it. I can follow his path, but on the rock there aren't any definite tracks to tell me much of anything."

"Except," Cassie said, "that the somebody didn't want to leave any tracks to be followed." She had an immediate sense of deep pleasure as she watched Johnny consider the point, and accept it. His quick smile was her accolade. She supposed she was being womanlike in pressing the advantage: "I want to go home, Johnny."

Johnny merely looked at her.

"No deep injuries," Cassie said, "nothing that needs a hospital. At home ——"

"No, *chica*. Not yet."

She studied him quietly. "So it *was* you. The doctor twisted and squirmed when I braced him."

"We don't know enough yet," Johnny said, "and I want you safe."

"You don't even know that what happened to me had anything to do with — warning."

Johnny shook his head. "The dead kid had fired a gun. He'd been to Lucy Carruthers' house the day she was killed. He'd been to your house that night. Now he's got himself dead. Don't tell me it's all coincidence, *chica.*" The white teeth flashed suddenly. "Because I won't buy it. But maybe there is a solution." He walked to the telephone and gave the switchboard an outside number.

Cassie watched, frowning.

"Ben?" Johnny said. "Johnny Ortiz here. How would you like a house guest for a few days? Cassie. To be looked after so nothing can happen to her?"

"Why, hell, yes." Ben's voice was a shout that carried clearly across the room. "And you may not get her back, boy. I'm not as young as I used to be, but, by God, there's still life in me. Bring her out."

Johnny hung up slowly. He was smiling. "You'll be safe with Ben, *chica.* Anybody who tries to bother you out there will get his head handed to him on a tin plate." He paused, smiling still. "You want help dressing?"

There was a moon; in the high thin air it was enormous and brilliant, filling the sky with light, casting the great mountains into shadow, coloring the mesa land itself almost as if with a blanket of snow.

They sat in the huge two-story living room. Three sides of the room were galleried; the fourth, against which the vast stone fireplace and chimney were set, was mostly glass, facing the mountains. "When I first came here," Ben

72

said, "a man did best without too much glass. Times you tended to feel naked at night when you walked past a window." He smiled. "Not many times, not nearly as many as they'd have you believe in movies or the TV, but some, enough."

Cassie watched the big old man, smiling. The funny thing was, she thought, he was not laying it on at all. There were tales, legends now, and most of them were true, about how men like Ben Hart started with nothing but their hands and their hearts and scrabbled and scratched and fought for what they could get, and hold. On the floor at her feet Chico dozed.

"But, hell," Ben said, "we're real civilized now, fences and black-top roads and fresh vegetables, even seafood flown in from God knows where." He was smiling broadly. "So I said, by God, I've always wanted to be able to sit here and look at those big damn mountains with a drink in my hand and a piñon fire going, so here she is, this room I always thought about."

The floors were polished brick spread with Indian rugs Cassie's museum director hoped would one day be in the collection he cared for with pride. The walls were whitewashed adobe with mounted heads – deer, elk, Barbary sheep, mountain goat, black bear, grizzly. There were paintings; great slashing colors against heavy grays and blacks and beige-browns of the land. "I don't know a damn thing about art," Ben would say, "but, by God, I've lived here, and I don't want any piss-washed city drawing that looks like somebody's park all neat and tended with all the edges trimmed. I want to see pictures of country that makes you sweat, that'll kill you of thirst if you aren't careful and then turn around in the next minute and drown you in a cloudburst romping down a dry wash or freeze you to death in its mountains."

"It's beautiful, Ben," Cassie said, and meant it.

Johnny said, "Only one thing." He was unsmiling. "Roads and fences and seafood, but things can still happen, Ben."

"I know it, boy." Ben's own smile was gone. "And I don't forget it, ever." He patted Cassie's knee. "How about another small hooker of bourbon, and then bed? You'll sleep tight. Nothing's going to bother you."

12

Tony Lopez perched on the corner of Johnny's desk. "You," Tony said, "and your goddam hunches." He looked at his notes. "Lucy Carruthers kept an appointment book. She had to. *"Dios!* the things that woman was mixed up in — the college, the museum, the opera, the garden club, the theater, the library, the Indian School and at least one art gallery, the hospital — and that doesn't even touch things like lunches and dinner and benefits for this and that and just plain evenings I guess you'd call social." He paused for breath.

Johnny nodded. He even smiled. "And if Lowell Carruthers is right, and I think he is, she probably raised hell in every one of those directions. The wonder is that somebody didn't shoot her a long time ago." He made a small gesture. "But where was she going that evening?"

Always back to the main point, Tony thought. He had watched Johnny tracking, and that same concentration was there, too; into a tangle of footprints and tire marks and hoof prints and God only knew what, but when he came out the far side he was ignoring everything else and always following the same prints he had followed in. "Old lady Martindale up Lejos way?" Tony said, "You know her? Apples and Angus cattle and that trout stream she always kept stocked for Buddy? You know the place?"

Johnny knew it. He was frowning now. The Martindale ranch was forty miles from Santo Cristo, some of the way mountain road, slow driving, say an hour and a half. "That's where Lucy Carruthers was going?" He paused, and the frown deepened. "But Lucy Carruthers and old Mrs. Martindale —" He shook his head. "One of those feuds."

"Read this," Tony held out a small, cream-colored envelope.

It was addressed to: Miss Lucy Carruthers, the Camino, Santo Cristo. Its postmark was Lejos. Inside, a single fold of heavy cream-colored note paper: "Dear Miss Carruthers: Mrs. Alan Martindale has not been well recently, and she has asked me to write this note to you. She feels that it is past time that an ancient misunderstanding should be cleared up, and since she is unable to travel herself, she would very much appreciate it if you would be generous enough to come to the ranch to see her the evening of Tuesday, May 12, at half-past eight for what she fervently hopes can be a reconciliation. Our telephone service is at best erratic, so we shall expect no reply. Mrs. Martindale very much hopes that your presence Tuesday evening next will be your answer. Very truly yours." It was signed with three initials, illegible. After the initials was added the phrase: "For Mrs. Alan Martindale."

Johnny finished reading. He turned the note over and found nothing more. He looked at Tony and waited.

"She had the date marked down in her appointment book," Tony said. His voice was expressionless.

Johnny nodded. "Go on." Although he thought he could guess what was coming.

"There's nothing wrong with Mrs. Martindale," Tony said. "She ate my ass out for bothering her." He paused. "And there's nothing wrong with her phone service. I

76

checked." He paused again. "And Mrs. Martindale said she never, underline *never,* would even have allowed Lucy Carruthers inside her front door if she had come and she did not, repeat, did *not,* either write or have anybody else write. such a note. 'And now, young man, if you have satisfied your vulgar curiosity . . .' " Tony sighed.

Johnny sat quiet and thought about it. "All right," he said at last, "now Don Hastings. What was he doing the night his studio was burglarized? Could you find that out?"

"Apparently he was bar-hopping."

"Apparently?"

"He was in at least one bar, and he was loaded when he came in. El Rincón. The bartender remembers the night because Hastings got into a fight and the bartender had to break it up."

"Who was he fighting with?"

Tony shook his head. "Some *turista.* Hastings claimed he was making a pass at the girl he had with him."

His English teacher back on the reservation would have thrown up her hands at the ambiguity of the sentence, Johnny thought, and was briefly amused. "The girl who was with Hastings, no?" And then, sharply now, "Who?"

"Sue Bright. She was with Hastings that night."

"She came into the bar with him?"

"And left with him. Nothing unusual about that. Sue Bright and Hastings are old friends."

"*Quizás.* Maybe." Johnny stared at the far wall. "The night his studio was burglarized," he said, "Hastings was with Sue Bright." He looked at Tony, who nodded. "And the night Lucy Carruthers was shot," Johnny went on, "the night when the Magnum had to be returned to Hastings' studio, if it was ever stolen in the first place – that night Hastings was with a girl named Tess, *and* Sue Bright." Pause. "Coincidence?"

Tony raised his broad shoulders and let them fall with an almost audible thud. "You tell me, *amigo.*"

"You look at a hand-woven rug," Johnny said. "The pattern keeps repeating itself. It's not always exactly the same, line for line, but the point is that the intention of the pattern *is* the same. Are you with me?"

Tony smiled, a wide, white-toothed, happy smile. "Since you ask," he said, "I'm nowhere near you. Lucy Carruthers gets a fake note. Don Hastings gets into a fight one night and passes out another." He shrugged those wide shoulders again. "A pattern, *amigo? Un poco loco,* seems to me."

"We're interested in four occasions," Johnny said, "and on each occasion the whereabouts of a specific person, or persons, and whether they were where they were by accident, or whether it could have been predicted that they would not have been home."

He paused and held up one hand, fingers spread to tick off his points. "First," he said, "is Don Hastings on the night his studio was burglarized. He was bar-hopping with Sue Bright. It's possible somebody knew he would be with her and wouldn't be coming home until late."

Another pause for emphasis. "Second, Lucy Carruthers. We know that somebody sent her a fake note. Why? Isn't it probable that the note was to get her away from her house, an hour-and-a-half drive each way? But she ran out of gas, and that blew it."

Tony tugged at one ear lobe. He was listening carefully now.

"Third," Johnny said, "that same night, Don Hastings again, and where he was and could it have been predicted." He paused. "Let's just assume, arguendo as the lawyers

78

say, that the Magnum had been stolen, and that after shooting Lucy Carruthers, somebody desperately wanted to get it back into Hastings' gun cabinet. His way was clear because Hastings was with Tess and Sue Bright, no? Is there a pattern?"

The goddam trouble, Tony thought, was that this goddam Indian held up facts and made them change shape right before your goddam eyes. Funny, he didn't resent it, but it was disconcerting. "What's the fourth occasion?" he said.

"Waldo Marks and his wife. Their house was burgled. Could it have been predicted that they wouldn't be home?"

His trouble, Tony told himself, was that he couldn't keep everything in mind at once. He had almost forgotten Waldo Marks. "The goddam Garden Club," he said. "They never miss a meeting."

Johnny nodded. "What about the rest of the recent burglaries? Where were the people whose houses were broken into, and could it have been predicted that they wouldn't be home? Get us enough occasions, and maybe we can see what the pattern is."

It made sense; Tony had to admit it. But he couldn't quite escape the feeling that he had been called to the principal's office to have the facts of life explained to him. "*Oigo,* I hear," he said, "*y obedezco,* I obey." He was sliding down from the desk when the commotion broke out in the corridor.

A female voice, Texas accent, said, "Take your goddam hands off me, fuzz!"

Johnny said without hesitation, "Bring her in here. That's Tess. I want to see what's up."

She was still barefoot, and wearing the hip-rider jeans and the tank top. Her long hair was uncombed, and she was breathing hard from exertion and anger. Wild would be the word, Johnny thought. The patrolman said, "We have a Wanted on her." His voice had the Spanish-American lilt. "She is only sixteen ——"

"And what goddam business is that of yours?" Beneath the thin fabric of the tank top her large breasts quivered with fury. She glared down at Johnny. "Or yours?"

"Maybe your parents want you," Johnny said.

"Screw my parents."

Tony Lopez said, "It's a thought." He was smiling down at the girl, a big man, easy and assured now, as he had not been before. He let his eyes drift down to her bare feet and back again to her face. "Maybe," he said, "they think you are *mucha mujer,* much woman, too much woman to be running loose just yet." His smile spread. "In their place, *guapa,* I would think the same."

Some of the fury had disappeared.

"What are you'all going to do to me?" the girl said.

Tony said, "What would you do, *guapa,* if you were fuzz?"

The girl shook her head and brushed back the long hair. "I suppose you'll bust every bar that served me a drink, just for openers."

Tony looked at Johnny. Johnny shook his head. "We'll make a few suggestions about ID cards, but we won't bust anybody. You don't look sixteen, and anybody can make a mistake."

The girl said, "But I suppose you'll bust Don because I'm a minor. You'll like that, won't you? He told me about you."

"And I told you," Johnny said, "that morals weren't my line. If I ever bust Don Hastings, it won't be because of you."

Tony said, "You see, *guapa,* we aren't quite as bad as advertised."

"What's this *guapa* bit?"

Tony's smile was very broad. "It's Spanish for very pretty girl with sex appeal." He paused. "Do you mind if I call you *guapa?*"

Tess looked down at Johnny. "Is he putting me on? About the Spanish, I mean?"

"I'd say," Johnny said, "that he gave you a very good idiomatic translation."

The girl brushed back her hair again. "Okay," she said, "maybe you aren't real creeps. But you'll call my home, won't you?"

"What would you do, *guapa?*" Tony was not treating her like a child but like a woman grown; he made no attempt to hide his admiration of her as a physical woman. "In our shoes?"

The girl's smile was sudden, and brilliant; it lighted her face, Johnny thought, like one of the local sunsets. "I'd call home," she said. "And they'd come and take me away and soon as we got home, I'd take out again just like last time, and the time before, and what good does it do?"

"Maybe they do it," Johnny said, "because they can't stop trying."

The smile was gone, but little of the original fury and resentment had returned. The girl was quite conscious of Tony; as with a restive mare and her trainer, his mere presence seemed to keep her quieted. She said, "They're, you know, square, real cubes. Responsibility and love and do-your-duty and all that crap. I'm me, and as long as what I do doesn't hurt anybody else, why can't I, you know, do what I want?"

It was hard not to smile. "And if what you do hurts them?" Johnny said. "Your parents? Your family?"

Tess brushed her hair back again with some of the old resentment. "That's different. I didn't ask to be born. It was their idea."

Tony said, "Come with me, *guapa*. We'll make that call, and then we'll see. Okay?"

The girl hesitated. She was still watching Johnny, searching his face for reaction to her last remarks. Johnny showed nothing. "Okay," the girl said, and turned away. At the doorway she stopped and looked back. "As fuzz goes," she said, "I guess you aren't so bad." That smile appeared again. "No Chicago thing. What's the matter with you, anyway?"

"We just aren't up to date," Johnny said. His smile matched her own. "You can answer a question for me, Tess." He watched her smile disappear. "Did Sue Bright ask you to pick Don up that first night, and take him to Sue's studio?"

The girl was silent for a few moments. She said at last, "If I tell you, will you let me go and forget about the phone call home?"

"Sorry." Johnny shook his head.

"Then why should I tell you? I'm no fink."

"Let me put it this way," Johnny said. "If you tell me, it won't hurt Don, and it may help him."

"That's a laugh." She was silent again, thoughtful. She glanced at Tony and then looked back again to Johnny. "What're you after, anyway? You're fixing to bust somebody, aren't you? Aren't you?"

"I hope so," Johnny said. "Somebody who's responsible for killing an old woman, beating another, a young, pretty one, killing a Spanish boy, and all of it just in order to steal things and make a few bucks. Do you like the sound of that?"

The girl seemed uncertain. "Don doesn't need to do that. He's loaded."

82

Johnny nodded. "Like I said, if you tell me whether Sue Bright asked you to pick up Don that night, it won't hurt him, and it might help him."

The girl brushed her hair back absently. She shuffled one bare foot. Decision came at last. "She didn't tell me to, exactly," she said. "She pointed him out and said he liked, well, you know" — she stopped and looked at Tony and broke out the full sunset smile — "young *guapa* girls. And, well, I, you know, let him see me and we had a drink, and then that bartender, the creep, threw us out, so I took him to Sue's, that's all." She was silent, watching Johnny's face.

"Thanks," Johnny said; and he smiled and added the magic word: *"guapa."*

13

Johnny sat in Doc Easy's office. "No identification in the boy's pockets," Johnny said, "and his prints aren't on file. Nobody's come in to report a missing sixteen-seventeen-year-old Spanish boy." He shrugged faintly. "Santo Cristo isn't New York, but forty, forty-five thousand people aren't easy to sift for the one who isn't where he's supposed to be."

"Maybe he's a stranger," Doc said.

Johnny shook his head. "He was at Lucy Carruthers' house the day or the evening she was shot. And he was at Cassie's house the night she was beaten. I know his footprints."

Doc Easy looked skeptical.

"Look," Johnny said, "put it this way. You see an operation, let's say an appendicitis scar. Could you recognize a particular surgeon's work? I couldn't, of course, but that's your bailiwick, not mine. Tracks are mine." He paused. "And that's what I wanted to ask. Any surgical scars we might use for identification, track down the surgeon who did the job, ask him?"

Doc shook his head. "Healthy boy. And with the diet he probably had, the diet many of them do have, don't ask me how he could be that healthy. No scars except minor cuts he'd have taken care of himself."

"Dental work?"

Doc made a braying sound that was intended as laughter. "If the only patients Santo Cristo dentists had were Spanish-Americans of lower-income level, they'd starve. Again, I don't know why, but it's a fact. The kid had all of his teeth, and not a single cavity or filling. Probably the local water has something to do with it." Doc shook his head. "I'm no help. Sorry."

Johnny stood up. "We'll find out who he was. I was just trying to do it the easy way. Now we settle down to hunt."

Johnny had pictures of the dead boy. To Tony Lopez he said, "He went to school sometime. Have somebody try the mid-highs and junior-highs, and if he didn't get that far, back to the elementary schools. He'll look different, of course, but maybe somebody will recognize him. And have juvenile court checked, and the state employment office, and welfare, routine." Wheels set in motion.

Lowell Carruthers came to see Johnny. In his easy, polite way he apologized for the interruption and offered the hope that his presence was not a burden. "I have been named as Cousin Lucy's executor, lieutenant. It was her wish that her body be buried in Boston." The corners of his eyes crinkled. "For forty years this was her home, but there is chauvinism deep in all of us."

Johnny agreed that it seemed to be so. He wondered what direction, if any, his own chauvinism might take, and decided he would rather not know. "I don't see why we can't release the body," he said.

"I appreciate your co-operation." Pause. "There are one or two interesting provisions in the will, lieutenant. The bulk of the estate, subject, of course, to some trust restrictions, goes to Donald who will, no doubt, squander as much of it as he can." Pause. "You are thinking what, lieutenant?"

"Cop's thoughts," Johnny said. "Hastings had better

not start spending that money in anticipation of having it. We may still find that he shot her."

Carruthers nodded. "And it is an established legal principle that one cannot benefit from his crime. I had considered the point, which is the main reason I am here. If Donald for any reason is unable to inherit, then the bulk of the estate goes to local organizations, including the museum, the opera, the hospital, the college library, and an organization I know nothing about, a kind of club established to keep young Spanish-American boys out of mischief." Carruthers paused. "The club is headed by a man named Billy Joe Harmon, and the sum of twenty-five thousand dollars would go to him without restrictions."

Johnny thought about it.

"Two comments occur to me, lieutenant," Carruthers said. "The first is that the wills of elderly spinsters frequently contain unusual bequests – money to found homes for stray cats, funds for psychical research, funds for the care and feeding of the town pigeons, that type of thing."

Johnny nodded. True enough.

"The second comment," Carruthers said, "is that I imagine murder has been committed before now for smaller sums than twenty-five thousand dollars."

"I know one," Johnny said, "that was committed for eighty-seven cents to buy a bottle of muscatel." He got up from his chair. "I think I'll have a talk with Billy Joe Harmon. Care to come along?"

Carruthers too was standing. "Delighted," he said.

Billy Joe Harmon was available. "It's one of the hazards of the profession, lieutenant, being idle. I can't sell nothin' at all unless I have at least a *pro*spective customer, and what with the condition of the stock market and the pessimism that seems to *pre*vail in the country, *pro*spective customers are few and far between." He smiled. "You wouldn't have brought me one now, by any chance, would you?" He looked with hope at Carruthers.

Johnny made the introduction. Billy Joe's smile disappeared. He shook Carruthers' hand. "A real fine lady, Miss Lucy," he said. "Her death saddens me, it does indeed. You have my sympathy."

Johnny said, "You knew her well, Mr. Harmon?"

"Billy Joe, sir, please. And I wouldn't say that I knew her well. She was a real lady, and I'm just a *auto*mobile salesman, but we did talk from time to time. I sold her her *auto*mobile, and when she brought it in for servicing — it never needed anything else — why, we chatted if she wasn't in a hurry to keep one of her engagements. She was mostly real busy, but she did find a few minutes from time to time to ask me about my boys — I call them my boys, but they really aren't, of course, you understand."

"Spanish-American boys," Carruthers said.

"Yes, sir. Some of them have jobs — I do what I can in that direction — and some do not. The important thing —" He stopped. He had, as Johnny had noted before, a variety of roles he could play with ease; he turned sheepish now, the zealot suddenly realizing that he has been carried away by his enthusiasm. "Miss Lucy was real interested," he said, "but that don't mean you'all are too."

Carruthers said, "Did Cousin Lucy aid you financially?"

"Yes, sir, in a way she did. She was real generous. I happened to mention what a fine thing a ping-pong table was to keep boys entertained, and that very afternoon here came a Sears truck delivering their very best ping-pong table with paddles and balls and a net — now wasn't that a fine, generous thing to do?"

A telephone rang inside the building, and a voice, hollow on the public-address speaker, called Billy Joe Harmon's name. "Excuse me," Billy Joe said. "I don't rightly think I'll be long."

"We may come back again," Johnny said. He and Carruthers walked out to Johnny's pick-up.

As they drove away Carruthers said, "Have you ever watched an experienced politician on one of those television meet-the-press shows, lieutenant? A question is asked. It disappears in a cloud of verbiage like smoke in a high wind. Mr. Harmon employs a similar evasive technique. A question concerning financial aid becomes the tale of a ping-pong table." He smiled in Johnny's direction. "I must say," Carruthers said, "that I admire his verbal agility."

"Let's take a look at the shed," Johnny said, "ping-pong table, and all."

Cassie was being treated, she thought, like a fragile thing, which she was not. "Relax and enjoy it," Ben Hart said. "Play princess in the tower." But he did understand; inactivity was anathema to him, too. "I'll take you for a ride in the chopper, honey. How about that? Fewer bumps in the air than on the ground to jar your bruises."

Cassie had never been in a helicopter before, and it was, she decided, like being in an elevated goldfish bowl, open and exposed to everybody and everything. There was in the beginning a sense of insecurity, but this quickly disappeared, and she had to admit that the view of the country was spectacular.

They flew over Cloud Mesa, which she had never seen from the air, and she looked down on the geometric grid lines of her own dig, temporarily abandoned now. "Until we get a new grant," she told Ben. "That's the story of every anthropologist's life: you go from grant to grant, with valleys of wishing in between." From the helicopter, seeing as she could never see even from a topographical map the total isolation of the mesa, she had the feeling that she was closer than she had ever been to the people who so long ago had chosen the mesa top for their home.

"I can see why they went there in the first place," Ben said. They were circling the mesa now. "Only that one way up to the top, easy to defend. But why did they leave?"

"We don't know, Ben. Maybe one day we'll find out." Maybe. One more little bit of knowledge to add to the world's store — assuming, of course, that the human race didn't destroy the world and its store of knowledge first; dismal thought. Cassie shook her head. Her smile was wry. "I have a case of the fantods. Show me that possible kiva you told me about."

They swung back over Ben's fence line, passed a stock tank and a dry wash, and then paused hovering over broken ground overgrown with chamisa, prickly pear, and cholla. Through the growth they could make out the faint outline of a circle too regular for a natural formation.

Cassie was all interest now, philosophical speculation set aside. "Could be, Ben," she said. "The roof collapsed. Dirt washed in. The vegetation took hold. I'd like to come out one day and poke around."

Ben smiled. "Better wear armor. My boy looked like he'd been through a meat grinder before he got that calf out."

The distant mountains were blue; white cumulus clouds riding above the taller peaks. In the foreground the hills seemed folded into secret shadows, and the brown flat land flowed around and past them, except for a single ribbon of highway unscarred for a hundred miles.

An automobile lifted a dust plume in this immensity of space. Cassie watched it. "Wherever he thinks he's going," she said, "he's in a hurry."

"There's nothing there," Ben said. "It's pueblo land, and the pueblo itself is way over yonder."

"Look," Cassie said, and pointed. A second dust plume was approaching the first on an intersecting course. Both began to slow, and in a moment both cars had stopped, close together; two men got out. "A conference," Cassie said. She was smiling. "At least their conversation won't be overheard."

There was a sudden glint of light. "But," Ben said, "they aren't taking any chances. I wonder why. He's studying us through field glasses." He glanced at Cassie. Alone, he would have gone to investigate just for the hell of it, but he had no right to take Cassie with him. Out in this broad country some men got a little touchy about being looked at too closely. "I want to check on another stock tank, honey," Ben said, "then we'll head back." As he banked the chopper away from the two cars, he caught a second flash of sunlight reflected from binocular lenses. Somebody, Ben thought, was interested, real interested in who they were and what they were doing. Some characters, like some horses, were real spooky . . .

The man with the binoculars watched the chopper until it was only a small stuttering speck in the distance. "That was old Ben Hart," he said.

The other man shrugged. "So?"

"That goddam black girl was with him, the nosy one." He laid the binoculars carefully on the seat of his car. "Johnny Ortiz snuffling around. Ben Hart and the black girl snooping." He shook his head, for the moment putting the matter aside. "All right," he said. "Let's get to

90

it." He unlocked the trunk of his car. "A real fine load of merchandise this time." He looked at the other man. "And," he said, "it's all inventoried, real careful. Just so there won't be any misunderstanding."

"You're a suspicious bastard." It was said without animosity.

"Careful is the word, friend." The man glanced again at the helicopter already far across Ben's broad holdings. "Careful," he said again. He was thinking of Cassie. "And a girl like her with brains and all can cause a man grief. So can that Indian Ortiz." He smiled suddenly. "Sometimes a man has to take what we called in the Army preventive action."

14

The shed was behind Montoya's wood-and-junk yard off the Camino. Johnny parked the pick-up beyond a pile of seven-foot cedar posts, hard by three old bathtubs, a tangle of dug-up gas pipe, and an irregular mound of used bricks. He was faintly amused at the care with which Lowell Carruthers picked his way through the litter; and he wondered if Miss Lucy Carruthers had ever actually visited Billy Joe Harmon's do-good project, to which she had bequeathed a possible $25,000.

A radio was blasting hard rock sound, and Johnny, smiling, said, "I think we follow our ears." He led the way.

The shed itself was of unpainted, unfinished board-and-batten, but the windows were intact, as Johnny thought they had not been a few months before, and a faded blue door had been hung in what he remembered as an open doorway. Over the lintel a crudely lettered sign read: *Esperamos.* "It can mean, 'We hope,'" Johnny said, "or 'We wait,' or even 'We trust.'" He glanced at Carruthers.

"Interesting ambiguity," Carruthers said, and let it go at that.

Johnny knocked on the faded blue door. Someone shouted, "Come in!" and another voice said, *"Adelante!"* Take your pick. When Johnny pushed the door open the blast of sound was almost painful.

There were four boys, sixteen-seventeen, Spanish-American, dressed almost to a pattern: tight dark trousers, light shirts, heeled, pointed-toe shoes. But one boy, Johnny noticed, wore boots, black and shiny, and, yes, alligator-grain, whether real leather or simulated, he could not easily tell. It was this boy who said, "Oh, God, fuzz." He reached to turn down the volume of the radio. "We making too much noise, dad? Is that the beef?"

Johnny shook his head. He looked around in open curiosity. There was the ping-pong table, paddles, and balls lying on it awaiting action. There were a broken-down sofa and half a dozen delapidated chairs. In the corner of the room a punching bag. On a table was a pile of magazines and some dog-eared paperbacks that were probably not recommended Sunday school reading or viewing material, Johnny thought; but, what the hell, he was not concerned with morals, and, anyway, pictures of naked females and stories of sex were perfectly legal and even fashionable these days.

At the far end of the shed was a partition and a closed door — Billy Joe's office, he supposed, if that was what you would call it; a place where records, receipts, and maybe some articles of minor value could be kept out of general careless use.

The boy with the boots was watching Johnny's face. "Well?" he said. *"Satisfecho?"* He grinned. "Behind that door is where we keep all the pot we smoke." The other three boys laughed. "And," the boy with the boots said, "it's where we lock up the chicks and, you know, torture them, torture the hell out of them. You want a game of ping-pong, fuzz?"

Johnny walked to the door and opened it. As he thought: a desk, four chairs, a filing cabinet; in the corner

93

a battered folding screen for slides or movies; four pitching horseshoes hung on a wall peg; the top of the filing cabinet was piled high with dusty papers. He was aware that Carruthers was standing right behind him, looking into the office with interest; and Johnny had an idea that Carruthers was not missing much.

The boy with the boots pushed through the doorway. He walked straight to the desk and pulled open the drawers, left them gaping. Then one by one he pulled out the drawers of the filing cabinet. Johnny didn't even bother to look; it was obvious there was nothing to cause comment. The boy slammed the drawers shut. "Okay," he said, "now what do you want, fuzz?"

"Just a visit." Johnny paused. "You're in charge?"

"Nobody's in charge. This is, like, a democracy, you know about that?" From the large outer room there was laughter; the chorus, Johnny thought, coming in on cue.

"Billy Joe Harmon?" Johnny said.

"He's different."

"How?"

"Cut it out, fuzz. Billy Joe is, like, a friend, you know what I mean? He's an Anglo, but what the hell, he's not like other Anglos with that kiss-my-ass look in their eye. You see this place? It was nothing, nothing, *nada*. He got the stuff and fixed the windows and put up the doors — and we watched him and wondered what the hell he was doing." The boy paused. "And then when he was done, windows in, lock on the door, he said, 'Okay. It's all yours, fellows. If you want it." He paused again. "You see what I mean?" No laughter from the outer room this time.

"In a way," Johnny said. Then, "How are you at pitching horseshoes?"

"I'll beat your ass. So will any guy here."

And, Johnny thought, they probably would, too.

94

"I'm glad to hear it," he said. He had no hunches, no tiny flickering doubt tucked away in the depth of his mind, nagging. He glanced at Carruthers again, and saw no doubts in his face either. "Thanks for the tour," Johnny said to the boy in boots.

The boy hesitated. Then, natural politesse asserting itself however grudgingly, *"De nada."*

"By the way," Johnny said, and his hand came out of his pocket with the picture of the dead boy. He held it out. "You know him?" He watched the boy's face carefully.

The kid was good; no doubt about that. But the picture caught him off-balance, and his eyelids shifted slightly, a muscle tightened in his cheek. He shook his head. *"No lo he visto,"* he said, *"nunca."* "I haven't seen him ever." He turned to the outer room and summoned his chorus. "You guys ever seen this *chico?"*

They crowded around. No foot shuffling, no muffled laughter; this was dead serious. One by one they shook their heads. The third and last boy said, "It looks like Felipe Martinez, but it isn't him. Never saw him before." He looked Johnny straight in the eye.

Johnny smiled and nodded. He put the picture away. "Okay, fellows. Thanks again." He looked at the boy with the boots. "What's your name?"

"Joe Baca. Why?"

Rhetorical question; Johnny ignored it. "You go to school, Joe?"

The boy's dark eyes watched him steadily. "You know better, fuzz. You even got a name for us, haven't you? I'm a drop-out. That means I'm a punk, don't it?" Pause. "Don't it?"

"But not to Billy Joe Harmon," Johnny said.

"That's right, fuzz." What had been reflexive

antagonism before was pure venom now. "You better believe it, too."

Johnny and Carruthers walked out into the bright day. The door closed behind them, and immediately the radio began to blare its hard rock sound. Carruthers said, "I visited the camp of North Korean prisoners of war at Panmunjon, lieutenant. I experienced the same miasma of hatred. You could almost taste it."

Johnny nodded. He was walking without haste toward the horseshoe court. It was well laid out: the stakes themselves were set in wood-outlined pits filled with raked clay; the area surrounding was smooth bare dirt. "I felt it," he said.

Carruthers said, "Was it because of me? Because I am – Anglo?" He paused and then said in that gentle polite way of his, "Do I have a kiss-my-ass attitude that shows, lieutenant?" He paused again. "I am quite serious."

"They see it," Johnny said, "whether it's there or not. I'm not sure I can blame them." He had stopped and was studying the ground of the court. "Except," he said, "when they lie to me." His voice was quiet.

Carruthers hesitated. "I'm not sure I follow you."

"The dead boy's footprints are all around here," Johnny said. "They knew him, all right. They pitched horseshoes with him."

It was, after all, merely a tedious, rather than a difficult, task to identify the dead boy. Someone was bound to recognize him; it happened to be a teacher. "Julio Romero," Tony Lopez said. "Went part way through junior high and said the hell with it. He's done odd jobs, no particular skills, pumped gas, worked as a mason's assistant but he didn't like that, worked for a time for a landscape gardener, and for the last year" – he

96

cocked an eye at Johnny — "he's worked two-three days a week for Miss Lucy Carruthers, mowing her lawn, trimming her hedges, weeding her garden, that kind of thing." Tony was silent, wondering what Johnny might make out of that.

"So now they're both dead," Johnny said. Was there a relationship between the two deaths? Almost certainly. And was the garden theme significant, or did it just keep popping up by accident — Miss Lucy's carefully tended garden, the Waldo Markses and their Garden Club membership, now the boy himself working as a gardener? Of course. Of course. "Two-three days a week at the Carruthers' house," Johnny said. "Where else did he work?" He saw that oh-God-here-we-go-again expression in Tony's face, and he smiled at it. "Not that complicated, *amigo*. Did Romero work, for instance, for Waldo Marks? For Don Hastings? For any of the others on your list whose houses have been burglarized?"

Silence. Then, "Yeah, sure," Tony said. When it was pointed out to you it was perfectly obvious, that was the maddening part. "We'll check it out." He paused. "That Anglo chick — Tess, her last name is Ronson, by the way, and her father and mother are flying up from Fort Worth in their own plane to get her. What makes a kid like that tick?"

"How would I know?" Johnny said.

"Kid has everything," Tony said, "so she shucks off her shoes and throws away her bra and shacks up with people like Hastings and Sue Bright." He shook his head. Then, watching Johnny's face, "What's funny?"

"You're a prude," Johnny said. "You, the scourge of the *barrio.*" It was a long time since he had felt like laughing aloud.

"She's sixteen," Tony said.

97

"Maybe she'll grow out of it."

"Yeah," Tony said, "if she lives long enough."

It was a sobering thought, and all at once the desire for laughter disappeared. "She's maybe mixed up in the whole business," Johnny said, and nodded. "Only on the edge, of course, if at all, but she's the kind who doesn't think anybody or anything will hurt her, ever." It was hard to keep down the annoyance (envy?) he felt toward someone who could take this view. "It's a beautiful world to her," he said, "and it's filled with beautiful people and she can pad through it barefoot and never even get scratched." He shook his head. "I want to see her parents when they get here."

And now it was Tony's turn to smile. "A *Texano,*" he said. "Owns oil wells and flies his own plane, and you're going to show him the light?"

"No," Johnny said. "I'm just going to see that he gets Tess baby out of here, and keeps her out until we get this mess cleaned up."

Don Hastings sat in Sue Bright's studio and stared at the nude pictures of Tess set in line on the picture rail along the wall. "San Quentin quail," he said and looked at Sue. "I could be in trouble up to here." He ran the edge of his hand across his throat.

Sue smiled. "Not Don baby." The smile spread. "And it isn't contributing to the delinquency of a minor or statutory rape Johnny Ortiz is thinking about."

There it was again, that cold emptiness in the pit of his stomach whenever he merely thought of Johnny Ortiz. "He knows I was here the night Aunt Lucy was shot."

Sue shook her head. "He knows I *say* you were here."

"So does Tess."

"Tess is going back home to Fort Worth." Up and

down Arroyo Road the Santo Cristo grapevine carried all local news with the speed of sight. "And there," Sue said, "goes half your alibi. She's made her statement, but you'll never in this world be able to get her back to repeat it."

Don was silent for a little time, thoughtful. "And that leaves you," he said at last.

"That leaves me."

That cold emptiness had returned to his stomach and it was difficult to keep his breathing steady. "Bad scene," he said. "Bad dialogue. They wouldn't even take it for summer replacement. What am I supposed to do now, ask what you're driving at?"

"These things happen," Sue said. She was smiling no longer. "People have to lean on each other. Sometimes it takes a little straining ——"

"What straining, for God's sake?" His voice was over-loud, but he couldn't help it. Somewhere he had read that everyone contained both male and female characteristics, and it was sure as hell true of this woman who was beginning to torment him: she could be pliantly, lovingly, excitingly female, as who knew better than he; but she could also, as now, show a kind of male toughness that was all the more frightening because it seemed out of context. "I was here. You know it. Where's the strain?"

"I don't know where you were before you came here," Sue said.

"I was with Tess. You saw me with her. You, goddam it, pointed me out to her. She told me." He had wondered why, but at the moment it didn't seem important.

"But before that?" Sue said. "How can I be sure of the time? You don't count the minutes in a bar. Or here. Maybe you and Tess didn't get here until, say, nine o'clock, or even nine-thirty, how can I be sure?"

He made himself sit quite still; sometimes it helped.

He said at last, quieter now, "Your point is that I could have killed Aunt Lucy, taken the gun home, then gone to the bar and been picked up by Tess and brought here?"

"Why," Sue said, "that's how it could have been."

"Do you think it was?"

"What I think doesn't matter a damn. It's what I say that counts, under oath if I have to."

There was a long silence. There were those nude photos of Tess, and now they seemed to mock him, because if it hadn't been for Tess he would probably have gone from bar to bar and lots of people would have seen him. Instead there was only this ambidextrous bitch to support him. And the gun *was* his. And he *had* reported it stolen, but there it was when Johnny Ortiz came around. And there too was that goddam statuette of Cassie Enright, and Ortiz hadn't thought that was funny at all. And Apaches, like elephants, didn't forget. Hastings said as calmly as he could, "What it means, I suppose, is that I'd better be nice to you, is that it? Very nice to you?"

"Something like that had passed through my mind," Sue said. She was smiling as she stood up. "Let's have a drink, Don baby."

15

Tony Lopez sat on the corner of Johnny's desk. He had his notebook open and he gestured with it as he swore softly and with feeling in Spanish. He said at last, *"Tú tuviste razón, como siempre.* You were right, as always." He waved the notebook again. "Every one, like you said, possible. Romero worked for the Markses. He worked for Don Hastings. That's the first thing."

It figured, Johnny thought: the dead boy kept turning up, leaving footprints here, there, working for three people who were burglarized. Was that why he was killed? Because he was too intimately involved? Possible, even probable. Should he lean on the boys at the shack about Romero? Later, maybe. "Go on."

"The Flemings," Tony Lopez said, "Somebody practically cleaned their house out with a moving van three months ago — while they were on vacation in Hawaii. The society column in the paper said when they were going and for how long."

"And," Johnny said, "they didn't bother to ask us to have somebody keep an eye on the house." He nodded in disgust. Some people didn't have the brains God gave a pack rat.

"Same with the Burkes," Tony said, "and the Jose C.

de Bacas — society page telling where they were going, and when."

"Basta," Johnny said. The pattern was plain, but where did it get them? He felt no sense of trimph in being right. Finding the trail was only a beginning.

"Romero's father wants to see you," Tony said. "He probably wants to make a gripe because we let his son get himself killed. He wouldn't talk to me."

Johnny nodded wearily. "Send him in."

The father was in his late sixties, a big, bent man with huge hands hanging out of the cuffs of his work shirt, a Diego Rivera painting in the flesh. He sat down, and began in Spanish, "Julio my son —" He stopped, studied Johnny's face, and slowly shook his head. "He was not a good boy, *señor.*" Simple, dignified statement of fact. "He lied. He stole. It is not right to speak bad of the dead. I know that. But, *señor,* I thought that you should know that Julio, my son, did things he should not have done, and it was because of these things that he was killed."

Johnny said slowly, carefully, "You know that?"

"Sí, señor."

"How do you know?"

"It has to be." Declaration of faith, unassailable. "Julio was punished."

"Do you know who punished him?"

The father shook his head. "I do not know, and it does not matter. He was punished. That is all. His mother will pray for his soul, and maybe her prayers will be heard, and maybe they will not. Julio is in the hands of God now." He looked down at his own huge hands spread helplessly. "I could do nothing with him, *señor.*" He looked at Johnny again, and in his eyes there was a plea. "I tried."

"I'm sure you did," Johnny said, his voice was gentle.

102

He stood up. "Thank you for telling me this."

Romero had risen too. "I thought that you should know."

Tony Lopez stuck his head in the doorway after Romero was gone. "What was it about? A gripe?"

Johnny shook his head. "He came to tell me it was all his fault." And now, he thought, I am hearing confessions, yet. At times it seemed that the world was mad.

He had two more parents to see on that day. This father was tall, lean, authoritative, wearing tinted shooting glasses and alligator cowboy boots beneath elegant frontier trousers. Johnny stared thoughtfully at the boots. "J. W. Ronson," the father said. "You're holding my girl." There was accusation in his voice. Then, as an afterthought: "This here is Linda Mae, my wife."

Johnny was standing. "Sit down, please." The *Texano* tended to raise his hackles, and so, of course, he was being overpolite. He waited until they were seated before he took his own chair. "Tess is your daughter?" Those alligator boots — something was scurrying around in the corners of his mind like a mouse half-seen in shadows.

"'Tess,'" said Ronson, "is my daughter, yes, lieutenant. Now just you tell me what the damage is, *in*cluding that long distance telephone call, and I'll write you a check and we'll be on our way."

Johnny said softly, "The damage. Yes, of course." And he left it there for a few moments of hard silence. Then, "In the first place, she's a possible material witness in a murder case."

"I don't believe it," Ronson said. "If you've trumped up —"

"And in the second place," Johnny said, still softly, but in a voice that carried, "she's a juvenile, but I could

103

throw some morals charges her way that might be a little hard to squirm out of."

Ronson's mouth was open. He closed it in silence. The muscles of his jaws began to work. "Just what are you saying, lieutenant?"

"Nothing," Johnny said, "that is news to you, I'm sure." He was watching the wife's face, and saw that it was so. "Yes, Mrs. Ronson?" By contrast with the simple honesty of Julio Romero's father, these people, he thought, were scum: arrogant, selfish, deliberately self-deluding. It was small wonder that Tess had decided to go her own selfish way.

"I surely don't know what you mean, lieutenant," Linda Mae said. Her smile was confident. She too wore tinted shooting glasses and tailored frontier trousers over polished calfskin cowboy boots. Neiman-Marcus came to mind. Her tone hardened. "I'm sure I am misunderstanding you. Tess is sixteen."

The hell with them, Johnny thought. He wasn't going to make it any more difficult for Tess, and maybe, just maybe, he could shock these two into some sense of reality. "Maybe you'd like a medical report?" he said. "Or testimony that would stand up in court?" And, remembering, "Or a collection of nude photographs of your sixteen-year-old daughter taken by one of our more prominent lesbians?"

The little office was silent. Linda Mae looked at her husband. J. W. looked at the floor and then at the far wall, and, in final reluctance, at Johnny again. "What are you fixing to do, lieutenant?" Arrogance and accusation set aside.

Johnny took his time. Both parents watched him, apprehension plain. "I'm going to turn her over to you," Johnny said at last. "You can take her home, and, I hope, keep her there." He stood up and opened the office door, beckoned Tony Lopez. "Give them Tess," he said. "Get a signed receipt." He looked then at the Ronsons. "Have a nice flight back to Texas."

He watched J. W.'s alligator boots striding down the hall. They reminded him, of course, of that boy out at the shack, Joe Baca. So? A Spanish-American kid and a *Texano* – where was the connection he was trying so hard to make? He would, he thought, be damned if he knew.

Will Carston had the means, and the time, to indulge his whims. "They have some new papers I want to look at down at El Paso," he told Sid Thomas. "Then there's usually something new to see at the folk art collection in Juarez —"

"What you mean," Sid said, "is that you figure you've been too long in the same place and that fiddle foot of yours is beginning to itch." He had a suck of oxygen from his portable bottle. "How long will you be gone?"

Will smiled. "Only three days, perhaps four. I'll want to go again next month when Willis at the university will be back from Madrid."

"Three-four days!" Sid said. "Next month!" He snorted. "I figure each *day* is going to be my last."

"I try to live each day," Will said, "as if I were going to live forever." He smiled again. "Maybe we are saying the same thing in different ways." He paused. "You wouldn't like to go?"

Sid shook his head. "Only one thing I'm scared of," he said, "and that's of dying someplace else than here."

And so, three days later, it was to Sid, rather than to anyone in officialdom, that Will made his telephone call from Juarez. And Sid, delighted to be involved in anything out of the ordinary, called Johnny Ortiz. Johnny came to Sid's studio.

"Will Cranston," Sid said, "is a snooper and a

snickler. You know about snicklers? They collect. And snoopers snoop. And there isn't anybody better at either one than Will Cranston. He's spent his life at it." He had a long pull at his oxygen bottle. "Silver," he said.

Johnny shook his head. "You've lost me."

"Snicklers," Sid said, "never forget. They see a thing, they remember it because they might want to collect it. Two-three years ago Will went to a dinner party. People he didn't know well, and after the dinner party didn't want to know well. Real horses' asses, I gathered, but Will's too polite to say so. Name of Marks, Waldo Marks, you know them?"

Johnny was beginning to see the light. He nodded, merely that. Let the old man tell it his own way.

"They had some nice things," Sid said. "Will, the snickler, noticed them all. And remembered them. The silver tableware, he said, was a pattern he had never seen before." Sid paused. "Well, he's seen it again. In a shop in Juarez. That's what he called to say. Looks to him like the whole Marks silver service." He sniffed oxygen again, and was silent.

Johnny went to the phone. He spoke briefly to Tony Lopez. "Okay," he said then, "ask the Juarez police to get in touch with Will Cranston. He's staying —" He looked at Sid.

"Sylvia's," Sid said. "He always stays there." He was pleased with the reaction his revelation had produced. He loved to see things stirred up. He waved the oxygen tube like a baton. "Go, go, go!" he said.

16

Sue Bright found what she wanted at El Tecolote y El
Gatito. The bar was not crowded, and Sam, drinking
coffee, had time for talk. "That kid with the party in the
corner," Sue said. "She doesn't look like she's enjoying
herself too much."

"I've been noticing," Sam said. There was no love lost
between herself and Sue, but neither had there ever been
open enmity. Sam, saloon proprietor, wanted to keep it
that way.

"Good-looking kid," Sue said. "Nice body."

"I've noticed that, too."

Sue tasted her drink, set it down. She said quietly,
casually, "I wouldn't be treading on your toes, would I?"

"Not mine," Sam said. "Help yourself." She moved
down the bar as new customers came in. Idly, as her hands
moved in the automatic motions of pouring and mixing
drinks, making change, she watched the girl with the party
in the corner stand up and leave the table, headed for the
ladies' room. Sam didn't even have to look to know that
Sue followed. Sipping her coffee fifteen minutes later, she
noted that neither the girl nor Sue had come back, which
was only what she had expected: there was a rear exit
from El Tecolote y El Gatito just a step from the ladies'

john. It was, Sam thought, no business of hers what her customers did as long as they didn't cause trouble.

The girl's name was Jill, and she was nineteen years old, with the kind of accent one associated with upper-middle-class New England — good schools, perhaps a year at Smith or Wellesley, and then sudden conversion to the drop-out-tune-in-turn-on syndrome, and who knew the reasons either real or imagined? She wore tie-dyed jeans and a boy's blue work shirt, and she was barefoot. "Honey," Sue said, "you don't even smell good."

The girl was standing in the center of Sue's studio looking around curiously. There was the row of nude photographs of Tess on the picture rail. Here was a blown-up photo-mural of Cloud Mesa real enough to touch; the great pile rising majestic and mysterious against the limitless sky. There were Indian rugs on the waxed flagstone floor. A piñon fire burned in the corner fireplace. Within this high-ceilinged, thick-walled room, the rest of the world did not exist. "Far out," the girl said. She gestured at the row of photographs. "You want to take pix like that of me?"

Sue was smiling faintly. "Something like that."

There was no hesitation. "Okay." Jill brushed back her long hair. "You got any grass?"

"All you want, but later. Let's get you clean first."

Jill looked at her. "You going to bathe me?"

"What do you think?"

Jill shrugged. "Suits me." She looked around again. "Some pad."

"Maybe you'd like to stay a few days."

For the first time the girl produced what passed for a smile. "It's an idea."

"If we get along," Sue said, and for that brief

moment the almost male strength Don Hastings had noticed showed itself.

Jill saw it too, and liked what she saw. "Far out," she said. "Let's see about that bath."

It was still well before midnight. The piñon fire, replenished, cast flickering lights and shadows from the corner fireplace. It was the only light in the room.

Jill, a fine Chinese silk robe partially covering her nakedness, was stretched out on the sofa. She held a hand-rolled cigarette carefully between thumb and forefinger and she smoked in deep inhalations, retaining the smoke in her lungs until her exhalations were almost colorless. There were the short stubs of four other cigarettes in the ashtray at her elbow. "You have good grass, Sue baby." She smiled in a dreamy, relaxed way. "You're far out in many ways."

Sue was in a large chair. She too wore a robe, and cared not that it had slipped from her thighs, or that her breasts were almost wholly exposed. She watched the girl. "You're pretty good yourself," she said. She smiled. "I didn't think I'd made a mistake." She paused. "I have a friend who'd be interested in you." Another pause. "In us."

Jill finished the last long inhalation and dropped the stub in the ashtray. "I'm floating," she said, and smiled. "This friend — male or female?"

"Male."

Jill smiled again in that relaxed way. "Suits me," she said. "Anything you say." The smile spread. "It's all experience, right?"

"Right," Sue said. She stood up from the chair and did not bother to wrap the robe around herself. For a moment she stood looking at the girl. Then, "I'll phone," she said, and walked out of the studio to her bedroom.

It took three rings before Don Hastings' voice answered.

"Are you alone?" Sue said.

"I'm alone." He recognized the voice, and he wanted, but did not quite dare, to challenge Sue's right to call him at this hour. The action smacked of dictatorial power.

"Are you sober?"

"That too," Don said. He allowed a little of his resentment to show. "So?"

"I think you'd better come down," Sue said. "I've got something that'll interest you." Pause. "Her name is Jill, and she's nineteen and very happy on pot — and other things." Another pause. "And she's anxious for experience." Her voice altered subtly. "You wouldn't want to disappoint me, would you, Don baby?"

There was silence, hesitation plain. Damn the woman, anyway. "I'll come," Don said, and hung up.

Sue hung up too and sat quietly for a few moments. One wall of the bedroom was mirror. She studied her reflection without expression. Then she lifted the phone and dialed a second number. To the voice which answered, she said merely, "He's coming." She hung up and went back out to the studio where Jill, still stretched out on the sofa was smiling dreamily at the ceiling *vigas.* "Don's coming," Sue said.

The dreamy smile spread. "Out of sight," Jill said.

A man stood in deep shadow in a clump of piñon and juniper across Arroyo Road from Don Hastings' house. He waited quietly, patiently, while light after light went off, leaving only a single light in the studio, and another in the rear of the house. Don Hastings, large in the dimness, came out of the enclosed patio, closed the gate carefully and walked to the carport. The engine of his car had an almost angry sound as he backed out, turned, and started down Arroyo Road.

The man waited, five minutes, ten. The car did not return, and nothing stirred in the night.

He crossed the road then, let himself into the patio, avoided the pieces of sculpture and went straight to the door. He had a key. It fitted easily. He let himself inside, closed the door, and went quickly about his work.

It did not take long. In ten minutes he was back across the road, whistling to himself as he walked to his own car parked two streets away. He saw no one. He hoped Don was enjoying himself.

17

Johnny drove the pick-up rattling over the cattle guard at the entrance to Ben Hart's ranch. It was eight miles to the ranch house, and Johnny, smiling, remembered that old Ben had threatened to kick one man's ass the whole distance just for making noises about blackmail. What he would do to anyone who even made a gesture toward Cassie didn't want thinking about. Johnny had seen Ben looking through the sights of a rifle at a wounded bear, a grizzly at that. There was no give in the old man, none.

The floodlights were not yet on at the main house when Johnny parked the pick-up, started for the door and then paused to admire the view. The great mountains, snow-capped still, were turning red – *Sangre de Cristo,* Blood of Christ, the early Spaniards had named them because of this glow. Will Carston had told Johnny once that in the Alps the same phenomenon was called *Alpenglühen.* Maybe one day, Johnny thought, he would see for himself; maybe he and Cassie together, wild pleasurable thought.

And here came Chico at a three-legged run, the splinted fourth leg touching the ground only occasionally. The little dog squealed his pleasure as Johnny dug fingers into his ruff. But Johnny's attention was on the doorway. Cassie was standing there, and that was the important thing. "Hi, *chica.*"

"Johnny." She seemed well and whole, rebounded from that beating. Maybe. There could be hidden scars. And instilled fear. He hoped not, because what he had to tell her was not going to be pleasant.

Ben Hart appeared in the doorway. "Come on in, stranger. I'm glad to see you. This female has been tearing my liver out at cribbage."

In the two-story living room, a crackling fire in the great fireplace and the last of the sunset glow fading from the mountains, Johnny said, "Anything happening here?"

Ben had a bottle and three glasses in his big hands. He set them down with care. "Nothing," he said. He poured three drinks, handed them around.

Cassie said quietly, "Are you expecting something, Johnny?"

"That's the hell of it, *chica,* I just don't know." He sipped his whisky, nodded his appreciation, and set the glass down. "We've identified the dead boy." He told them about it. "Nobody knows him from his picture, not even the kids he pitched horseshoes with." He shrugged. "That could be pure reflex. Probably was." He shook his head. "At the moment I don't see any point in leaning on them. They'd just close up tighter." He leaned back in his chair, here in this big room with these two people easier, more relaxed than he had been in some time. "So," he said, "what do we have?" He held up his hand, fingers spread, and ticked off the points on his fingers as he talked.

"One dead woman," he said. "Shot. With Don Hastings' gun that he had reported stolen, but that was in his gun case that next morning. Second: you, *chica,* beaten. Third: a kid nobody wants to admit knowing shot, killed." He looked at Ben. "With one of those over-powered .22's, at a hundred yards from a prone position — shooting fish in a rain barrel." He paused. "Don Hastings has a .220 Swift. I saw it in his gun case."

113

Cassie made a small movement and then was still. "I can't see him as Mack the Knife," she said.

Johnny nodded, "Neither can I. At the moment." Pause. "Now a telephone call from Will Cranston in Juarez. The Waldo Marks silver service, rare, expensive, stolen a week ago here, turns up down there in an apparently reputable shop." Another pause. "But that isn't the whole thing." He sipped his whisky and set the glass down. "Anonymous phone calls —" He shook his head. "Mostly from cranks, of course, and some not anonymous. We've got a woman, Anglo, who keeps swearing a neighbor is interfering with her television reception by operating a spy radio transmitter." The white teeth flashed. "There is no transmitter, but she doesn't believe it; she says it's just that spies are too smart for us, and maybe they are, how the hell do I know?"

Cassie, smiling, said, "Go on. You had an anonymous phone call that wasn't from a crank?"

Beautiful *and* bright, Johnny thought, and returned the smile with a nod. He did not feel like smiling. "This one said that if we looked around Don Hastings' house we'd find some things that were pretty interesting; he said Don boasted about them one night in a bar."

Ben held his glass almost hidden in his big hand. "What kind of things?"

"We asked, but the caller hung up." Johnny shook his head. "Male, female, Spanish, Anglo — without a tape of the voice and maybe oscilloscope examination, who could tell?" He paused again, and his face was expressionless. "One other thing the caller said." His voice was soft with anger. "It said not to overlook that statuette of you, *chica,* which is the part I don't like. It brings you back in."

Cassie closed her eyes briefly. When she opened them, both men were watching her. To Ben she said, "It's a nude statuette of me, Ben. I posed for it. No argument." Then,

114

to Johnny, "It was before I even knew you. It ——"

"*Chica,*" Johnny said, and his voice now was gentle, "we started from scratch one evening after a picnic, remember? What went before wasn't important. I couldn't care less about the statuette, or you and Hastings back then." Nearly true; near enough. Pause. Smile. "Believe me." The smile disappeared. "But whoever made that phone call made a point of the statuette, and that brings you right back on stage, and that's what I don't like."

There was quiet. In the great fireplace the burning logs crackled softly. The mountains had faded into purple shadow. All at once, automatically, the floodlights came on, throwing fences, out-buildings, Johnny's pick-up, and bushes of chamisa, clumps of prickly pear, and tortured canes of cholla into sharp focus. No-man's land, Johnny thought approvingly.

Ben said, "Did you follow up the call?"

Johnny nodded. "Hastings said he had no objections, so we didn't bother with a search warrant. Then he began to scream when we found a couple of silver trinkets that are on the Waldo Marks stolen list, and a couple of pieces of jade that came from the Lucy Carruthers house." He spread his hands. "He says he never saw them before, and he hasn't any idea how they got there." Pause. "He's running scared, and I don't blame him. The hand gun was his. The rifle that killed Romero could have been that .220 Swift of his. He is Lucy Carruthers' major heir. Now these things to tie him to the burglaries ——"

Cassie said, "Was the statuette there?" Her face and her voice were too unconcerned.

Johnny shook his head. "I asked Hastings where it was. He said he hadn't noticed that it was gone. Maybe yes, maybe no."

"And," Ben said, "if it turns up in Juarez too, what'll you think then?"

Johnny shook his head again. His voice was quiet. "It won't turn up in Juarez or anywhere else." He looked at them both. "It turned up in my office this afternoon, in a box sent through the mail." He left it there for a moment, unfinished. Then, "The head," he said, "had been cut off with a hacksaw. So had both breasts." A long pause. The muscles in his jaws worked. "That's why I want you here, *chica*. Somebody's playing rough."

Johnny drove the eight miles out to the highway from the ranch house, rattled over the cattle guard and then, on impulse, turned left instead of right, away from town, and he could not have said why. A few miles down the highway he turned off on a dirt road, stopped the pick-up, switched off engine and lights, and got out to stare at the great truncated mass of Cloud Mesa showing as an empty black shape against the star-filled sky.

The night was cool, but no wind stirred and the temperature was not uncomfortable. The land had a fragrance, undefinable, compounded of the odors of earth, rock and plants — cactus, chamisa, piñon, juniper, Apache plume, the early blossoms of flowering vetch and desert verbana. No lights showed, and against the total silence a coyote began to sing. Johnny listened, smiling. "Good hunting," he said, as the coyote's song came to a yapping end.

He, Johnny, had no purpose in being here. There was nothing to see in the darkness; in the silence nothing to hear. Still he stayed looking at the towering mesa, at the stars beyond it, billions of them like bright dust in the black sky; one hundred billion stars, he had read, in our galaxy alone.

Once upon a time man had thought himself and his earth the center of the universe. At least some men had; but it was difficult to see how in this immensity anyone

116

could ever have thought of himself as anything but insignificant.

The coyote started up his song again. Others joined him, a yapping, trilling chorus in the night to bring ranch dogs out of their sleep to pick up the ageless argument between the domesticated and the free. They hurled insults, Johnny thought, with almost human abandon. But they lacked human viciousness.

Men and rats, he had read once, were the only vertebrates that would deliberately destroy their own kind. Destroy, mutilate, threaten — the dismembered statuette was very clear in memory; its message plain: this time a piece of cast bronze; next time the flesh of the woman herself. Why else the emphasis in the anonymous phone call on a statuette Cassie had posed for?

The coyote chorus tapered off into silence. Distantly a dog continued to bark, but at last his voice, too, was stilled. There was the mesa, and there the stars, unchanged, unaffected. Johnny turned away, got into the pick-up and drove back to town.

His sleep that night was uneasy and filled with dream sequences he later could not recall. Well before dawn he awakened, listening, but the only sounds were the faint whisper of a breeze in the piñons, and a sudden scurrying that could only have been a field mouse or a ground squirrel hurrying to safety; and, as if to corroborate the analysis, an owl hooted nearby. Then there was quiet.

Through the bedroom window he could see the black sky still filled with stars, Orion's belt, Rigel and Betelgeuse dominating the scene. Star patterns were easy. If a star pattern baffled you, you could go to a book and identify it; simple as that. But human patterns were something else again, and in identifying them, or supplying them with motivation, which amounted to the same thing, books

117

were of scant, if any, value. Discovery had to be largely through what he supposed the head-shrinkers would call empathy. And in the black predawn that concept triggered a kind of response. He lay still, staring up into the darkness.

Slow, he told himself, slow and easy; don't try to overpower the thought. Where is the beginning?

Strangely enough, the beginning that came to mind was Tess. Why? Skin-tight hip-rider jeans, full young breasts bouncing in that tank top; long hair, bare feet; sixteen years old and playing both sides of the street with a combination of Sue Bright and Don Hastings; Texas oil man father, brushed-up dominant-type arrogant mother — why Tess as a start for understanding?

The answer did not appear, and he put the question aside for the moment. All right; what thrust itself forward next?

Those kids out at the shack, pitching horseshoes, playing ping-pong, reading dog-eared lurid paperbacks and leering at sex magazines, snarling at him, Johnny, just because he was Authority, lying to him about the dead boy — what possible connection was there between them and Tess? Except, of course, of course, the common distrust of, and resentment toward, the Establishment? Whatever the hell the Establishment was. Better, he thought; much better. Now what comes up?

Cassie. Inevitable. Cassie smiling, Cassie grave; Cassie clothed, Cassie naked, Cassie in miniature in that mutilated bronze statuette, Cassie lying beaten in her own house. Careful, he thought; anger won't help; go back and start over.

Tess, those *chicos* at the shack, the dead boy, Cassie — no, what *happened* to Cassie, and what the mutilated statuette threatened, that was how Cassie fitted into the equation.

118

Now, he thought, he was beginning to get the picture of a particular kind of mind at work. There is something you want? Hijack an airplane and hold the passengers hostage unless your demands are met. You object to a college ruling? Bomb the joint. The police (pigs) are being so unfair as to hold some of your terrorist chums? Kidnap a couple of officials and threaten to kill them unless your pals are released. Your aspirations are just; therefore whatever means are justified. End of thought-train.

It wasn't much, he had to admit, but it was something, and it separated some of the wheat from the chaff. Simple defiance of authority was not enough. Tess, those *chicos* at the shack, scratch them. Theirs was *reaction* rather than action initiated. *Unless they were directed.* Pause. Remember that one. As Tess may have been directed to pick up Don Hastings. As those *chicos* may have been directed? In what? By whom? And why did alligator boots come to mind again? Alligator boots? The Spanish kid and the Texano? What connection?

"Juan Felipe, *estúpido!*" He said it aloud. *"Seguro que sí!"* Alligator boots were expensive, expensive as all hell, a pair of handmade Tony Lama alligator boots cost an arm and a leg, and were just the kind of thing a *Texano* with oil wells would sport, but what about a Spanish kid here in Santo Cristo? *If* his boots were real, of course, and the chances were that they were not, but it was something that ought to have been checked out some time ago. Because if the *chico*'s boots were real alligator, then something was rotten in the *barrio,* and maybe at last a real trail was beginning to appear.

"Basta," he told himself. Nighttime thoughts were sometimes helpful, but they could be carried too far in wrong directions. He closed his eyes and made himself relax. His last waking thought was of Cassie, and later he wished he could remember what it was.

18

Lowell Carruthers, driving a rented automobile, drew up in front of Ben Hart's ranch house. He got out, looked around, at the view, at the buildings; and was impressed. Ben Hart met him at the top of the portal steps. "I hope," Carruthers said, "that I am not intruding?"

A funny little eastern fellow, Ben thought, but Johnny Ortiz had spoken up for him, and now that Ben looked a little closer he thought he saw what Johnny meant: like horses, some men had bottom and some did not; he could see that this one did. "Glad to know you," he said, and enveloped Carruthers' hand in his own. "Cassie's inside." He led the way.

Carruthers was impressed again. He had heard about Cassie, but never seen her. He made a small bow now over her hand. "The picture one conjures up of a female anthropologist," he said, "features glasses and thick ankles and, if I may say so, a face nowhere near as lovely as yours."

"Also white," Cassie said, and wondered why she was reacting defensively. Because Johnny and this man obviously got along, and perhaps she might not? Jealousy? Or was she just uptight? She had dreamed about that mutilated statuette, and awakened right on the verge of a scream.

Nothing in Carruthers' face had changed; and the

faintly nasal tenor voice was unperturbed. "I don't blame you for being skeptical, doctor. In your place I should probably have gone around the bend long ago." He thought of that Spanish boy at the shack speaking of Anglos who had that kiss-my-ass look in their eyes. He was learning, he thought; or he hoped he was. When a man was beyond learning, he might as well be dead. Better. "I understand," he said, "that my late cousin had managed to cut off funds for your Cloud Mesa excavations."

Cassie hesitated. Slowly she nodded. She could recall vividly that scene with Johnny when he had told her that Lucy Carruthers was dead and that her opinion of Lucy Carruthers was better kept to herself. She wondered now what direction this little man was heading.

"May I ask," Carruthers said, "the amount that was to have been made available?"

Cassie looked at Ben. Ben said merely, "Johnny sent him."

Cassie nodded then. "Between twenty and thirty thousand dollars," she said. "The exact amount to be allocated was under discussion." She paused. "Last summer's work came to just under twenty-eight thousand dollars."

Carruthers said slowly, "It must have been a disappointment when cousin Lucy intervened."

Disappointment? Cassie managed to smile. "Something of an understatement," she said.

Carruthers was silent, contemplative. He said at last, "Would it be too much to ask to see the excavation site?"

Again Cassie looked at Ben. Ben shrugged. "If you want to, honey. If you feel up to it." He saw decision in her face. "You better take the jeep. That's no place for a showroom car."

Carruthers drove. He seemed at ease in four-wheel

121

drive on rough terrain. Cassie said as much.

Carruthers produced his faint, deprecatory smile. "Guadalcanal," he said, "Korea, among other places. Jeeps and I are old friends."

They left the car and Cassie led the way up the single path to the mesa's top. In places the soft volcanic rock had been worn by climbing feet to a depth of ten or twelve inches, and at times the path was only one footprint wide. In all the centuries of the mesa's contact with humanity, Cassie wondered, had it ever been climbed before by someone like Carruthers, in a neat summer suit, a bow tie, polished, but now dusty, black loafers?

"Just be careful where you put a hand on a rock ledge," she said. "There are snakes." She glanced over her shoulder, and saw Carruthers' polite nod of acknowledgment. He was conserving his breath, she saw, and she approved. At seven thousand feet, and at his age, climbing would not be easy. But he did not lag behind.

They reached the top at last, and there, at the head of the path, they stopped to catch their breath. Carruthers looked around at the view, and slowly shook his head. "Unbelievable," he said.

To the north and east the mountains rose in tangled mass, stretching to infinity, their tops snow-covered, above timber line. To the north and west a single line of green — cottonwood trees — marked the river. Behind the river rose an isolated mountain mass; and to the south and west another. Between the two, purple with distance, but in this high dry air in plain view, was another single mountain etched on the horizon, and Cassie, smiling, pointed to it. "Mount Taylor," she said. "It's a hundred miles away by air."

Carruthers shook his head; and something like an angry bee passed between them. The whip crack that followed lagged well behind.

Cassie stared. Carruthers reacted. He seized her arm. His grip was astonishingly strong. "Quick! Out to the center!" Together they ran. A second whip crack sounded, but they did not hear the bullet's passage.

The gridlike excavations, slit trenches, near the center of the flat mesa top; Carruthers jumped in, and Cassie followed. Carruthers looked around. Their view of the ground below was blocked by the mesa edge. He nodded, satisfied. "We can't see down," he said, "and so it follows that no one can see up. We are safe here." He paused, watching Cassie's face.

"Unless someone with a gun comes up the path," she said. Her voice sounded calm enough, she thought, and wondered how that could be. "If someone does come up —" she said, and left the sentence unfinished. What was it Johnny had said only last night to Ben? "Shooting fish in a rain barrel."

"We are sitting targets," Carruthers said, "with nothing but rocks to throw." He nodded. He seemed unperturbed. "I am sorry, my dear. I had no idea." He even smiled. "Apology does seem inadequate." He glanced in the direction of the path. "While we wait to see if he does come, perhaps you will tell me a little about these excavations."

Cassie opened her mouth and closed it again carefully. It was unreal, she thought; the situation, and Lowell Carruthers, both. She said, "A lecture? Now?" Unbelieving.

"What better time?"

Again she opened her mouth, and again closed it soundlessly. Some of the tension seemed to flow from her body and her mind, and she could not have said how, or why, but it was so. She could even smile. "Very well," she said, and her voice was professionally calm now. "We know the people who lived here, but we are not sure where

123

they came from, or why they left. With this dig we hope to answer both those questions."

Carruthers merely glanced in the direction of the path. "And then?" he said, and smiled politely at Cassie. "Then," he said, answering his own question, "a little more knowledge will have been added to the world's store, is that it, doctor?" He nodded, and looked around at the dirt and rock.

Cassie stooped to pick up a small triangular object, and held it out for Carruthers to see. It was coral in color, and across its broad end a thin black line wavered in minute pattern. "Tenth, perhaps eleventh century," she said. "And not from here. There is no red clay here, and so the pot this was once a part of came from somewhere else, perhaps traded, perhaps stolen. With little bits and pieces like this, we try to reconstruct the past."

Carruthers took the shard and held it carefully. He was nodding in his quiet, polite way, and then his head came up to a listening attitude. Cassie heard it too: the sound of a car engine suddenly gunned into speed. They looked at one another. "Our friend," Carruthers said, "departing, I hope."

Cassie let her breath out in a long sigh. She was suddenly aware that she was aching all over from strain; and the pain of her strapped ribs, for days now almost forgotten, had returned. Up here on the mesa, she knew, sound played tricks, and one had to go right to the edge to know what was happening five hundred feet below. But she felt easier as she listened to the engine's sound, and she clung to the thought that it did indeed mean what Carruthers had said — the departure of the man with the rifle. She closed her eyes.

Carruthers said, quite calmly, "Perhaps I was premature." Merely that.

124

Cassie opened her eyes and stared at the top of the path. A man's head had appeared, and she squinted against the sun to try to make it out. Then the man himself appeared, rifle in hand, and she could have fainted in sheer relief. "Johnny," she said, "Johnny!"

He was unsmiling as he walked toward them in that steady, relentless pace of his. "It's all right, *chica.*" He looked at Carruthers. "But if I'd known you were going to bring her here, out in the open —" He shook his head.

"Foolish, perhaps, I admit, lieutenant," Carruthers said. He seemed to be making a decision. "But I did want to see what I am going to sponsor." He looked down at the coral-colored shard in his hand. Then he looked at Cassie. "You shall have your funds, doctor. I will not allow cousin Lucy's malevolence to reach out from the grave."

Single-file down the one path, Carruthers leading, Cassie in the middle, Johnny with rifle bringing up the rear. "I called Ben," Johnny said. "I wanted to talk to you, *chica.* He told me where you'd gone, and I didn't like it, so I came along. Somebody saw my dust trail and took off like a scalded cat. Too far to make out anything."

They had reached the bottom of the mesa now. Cassie turned to look up. She pointed, and shivered. "We paused at the top." Standing there, she thought, they had been clear targets against the bright sky. "Someone shot at us." She shivered again.

"Two shots, lieutenant," Carruthers said. "Only the first was close. We retreated to the excavations." He paused. "I saw no one. I saw no car. We were admiring the view."

"The car," Johnny said, "was parked around the angle of the mesa. On foot he had plenty of cover. I'll look around." He started off in that steady pace, rifle in hand,

125

head bent slightly forward, eyes on the ground.

Carruthers watched, and shook his head, smiling faintly. "I think," he said, "that I would rather not have the lieutenant on my trail." He took Cassie's arm. "We might as well sit in the jeep while we wait."

Johnny was not gone long. His face was expressionless when he returned. "Too many tracks to make any sense," he said. "Car tracks, footprints, empty cartridges —" He shook his head, and then smiled at the disappointment in Cassie's face. "I'm a tracker, *chica,* not a magician, and I don't know what tracks I'm looking for." The smile disappeared. "But sooner or later, I'll find out." He walked to his pick-up, put the rifle in its rack. "You lead," he said. "I'll follow you back to Ben's."

19

"Joe Baca," Tony Lopez said, "has no alligator boots. He says. Those pointy-toe Beatle boots, yes. Well worn. Why do the damn things always run over to the side?"

"Because," Johnny said, "the kids don't walk, they strut." He was thinking of Julio Romero's tracks leading to his broken body lying in the dirt. "Okay, Tony. Thanks."

Tony hesitated. "You made a mistake?"

"No," Johnny said, "I didn't make a mistake. Carruthers saw the boots too." He was silent for a few moments. "And that means," he said, "that Joe Baca got rid of the boots he was so proud of." Applying now the result of those night thoughts: "Because somebody told him to. Somebody with authority. At a guess, a fellow named Billy Joe Harmon." Little pieces fitting together. Maybe. He looked at Tony. "Yes?"

"Don't expect me to follow you," Tony said, "fellow who sees visions." He looked at the paper in his hand, happy to change the subject. "Juarez police have come up with quite a bit of the stuff on the Waldo Marks list, maybe half of it." He looked at Johnny. "That's pretty high percentage."

Johnny nodded. He pushed back his chair and stood up. "Maybe somebody is getting careless." He smiled wickedly. "I think I'll stir things up. Who knows what might crawl out of the brush?"

"Maybe a bear," Tony said, "or a rattlesnake. Be careful."

For effect, Johnny took a police car instead of the pick-up. First stop the shack behind Montoya's wood-and-junk yard. He left the car engine running, and the radio turned on. The hard rock music blasting out of the shack drowned the car radio at first, but when Joe Baca turned the music off, the flat, emotionless voices on the police wave length were clear, and Johnny could see that the kids listened, and were affected.

There were only three this time; as before, they were dressed in what almost amounted to a uniform: Beatle boots, tight black trousers, light-colored shirts. As before too, Joe Baca seemed in command. "Oh, God," he said, "fuzz again."

Before he had been affable; now he was subtly menacing. *"Amigo,"* Johnny said, and the way he pronounced the word gave it contemptuous bite. "I will do the talking. Outside, all of you."

The two other boys looked at Baca. Baca opened his mouth, and then closed it again when Johnny said, "I told you I would do the talking. Outside."

Baca hesitated, shrugged, and strutted through the doorway. The other boys followed. They stopped in a group and looked at Johnny. "Now what?" Baca said. It was a sneer.

"Now walk," Johnny said. "You. Alone. Over to the horseshoe pit and back."

"I don't get it."

"I said walk." And for a moment the clash of wills was plain between the man and the boy; but the moment passed quickly.

Baca shrugged again. He strutted, toes turned out,

128

shoulders in exaggerated motion. The two other boys watched him go, stop at the edge of the pit, turn and come back, smiling. He reached the group and stopped, looked at Johnny, smiling still. "So?"

Johnny paid no attention. He walked along the toed-out tracks, his eyes on the ground, turned and came back. Then he looked at Baca and nodded. He pointed to a second boy. "You. Walk."

The boy was frightened; that much was plain. He looked at Baca, who smiled no longer. He looked again at Johnny. He swallowed. *"Mire,"* he said, "look, I don't –" He stopped. Capitulation. He took a deep breath and walked quickly over to the pit and back. His tracks were plain in the dirt. He stood watching fearfully as Johnny followed the tracks, at one point bent to study them; and then returned. The flat voices on the police radio continued from another, colder world.

"Now you," Johnny said to the third boy, and this time there was no hesitation. The boy walked, almost ran, to the pit and back and then stood very still, his mouth working and his eyes round with fear as he watched Johnny go through his investigation.

Johnny walked back slowly. He looked at them all, but longest and hardest at Joe Baca. "So now we know," he said, and turned away, got into the police car, and closed the door with a solid thud. He let them see him pick up the microphone and speak into it. Then he hung it up and the emotionless voices resumed as he drove out of the wood yard.

The boys watched him go. It was Joe Baca who spoke. "Son a bitchin' fuzz," he said. His voice was not quite steady. He looked at the three double rows of footprints in the dirt. "Son a bitch!" he said again. *"Hijo de puta!* Who the hell he think he is?" He looked again at

129

the tracks, and then at the other two boys.

There was no answer.

Next stop up Arroyo Road at Don Hastings' house. Hastings himself opened the door, and for a moment defiance flickered. "What do you want?"

"A little talk," Johnny said. "Here, or down at headquarters, it's up to you."

The defiance died. The formidable mustache seemed to droop. "Oh, hell, come on in." And in the large studio room, "Drink? Or don't you official types ever unbend?"

"No drink." It was obvious that Hastings had already had a few. Johnny wondered if there was a reason. He walked over to the gun case, conscious that Hastings watched him. The 30-06 was there, along with the Browning over-and-under, and the double-barreled Parker. Johnny turned slowly. "Where's the Swift?"

Hastings was pouring himself another drink. "Right over there." He gestured toward the sliding door that led out to the portal facing the arroyo. The rifle lay across the arms of an easy chair.

Johnny walked over to the door. There were cottonwoods in the arroyo, and through the open spaces between their trunks he could see an almost vertical dirt bank cut by generations of flash floods. Mounted in front of the bank was a post and a small white target. Johnny picked up the rifle and squinted through the scope. The black center of the target sprang into sharp focus. He counted three holes in the ten-ring. "Good shooting." He laid the rifle on the chair arms. "Hundred yards. Flat trajectory."

"So?" Some of Hastings' defiance had rekindled itself. "I qualified once as expert rifleman. Can you make something of that?" And then all at once, as before, the defiance collapsed. "Look," Hastings said, "try being

130

human for a change. Every time I turn around there's something new that points at me. It was in the paper, the kid shot south of town, probably with a rifle like that. Why would I ——"

"He worked for you," Johnny said, and watched Hastings flinch as from a blow. "Every time *we* turn around," Johnny went on relentlessly, "there's something new that touches you, and if you think we're going to ignore it all, you're sillier even than you seem to be." It was not difficult to instill anger into his voice; the anger was already there, smoldering in his mind. "You say you're being framed. All right, by whom, and why?"

Hastings seemed to have forgotten the drink in his hands. "I don't know."

"Sue Bright?"

"That ambidextrous bitch."

Johnny was silent, thoughtful. He said in a quieter voice, "She sent Tess after you. Did you know that?"

"Yes."

"Do you know why?"

"How the hell would I know? Maybe just to get me mixed up with sixteen-year-old jail bait."

Maybe; maybe not. "Tess has gone back to Texas. No charges."

Hastings looked at his glass, raised it, and then in sudden impulse set it down hard, untouched, on a nearby table. Liquor splashed. He ignored it. "She's got another one now. Sue, I mean. Name of Jill. Nineteen years old." He paused and his voice changed. "Grew up in Brookline." Another pause. "I know her family. She knows mine." He was sober now. "How do you like that?"

"Not much." Johnny's voice was cold.

"Well, goddam it, it isn't my fault."

Whatever that meant, Johnny thought. "You're just

131

the innocent bystander again, is that it?" There was disgust in his voice now. "God help us," he said. "A remittance man with a conscience. You don't even have the courage of your vices. You make me want to puke." He started for the front door.

"You goddam Indian." It was a new Hastings voice.

Johnny stopped, turned. Hastings had the rifle in his hands, waist-high, his finger on the trigger. The muzzle was steady, pointing straight at Johnny's stomach. "You can't talk to me like that," Hastings said.

Johnny kept his eyes on Hastings' face. "I just did. I'll repeat it: you make me want to puke." He turned away then, opened the door, walked through, and closed it firmly. The flesh of his back was crawling all the way to the street and the waiting police car. Inside, he closed the door and let his breath out in a long sigh.

Two down, he thought, and two to go. It looked as if he was indeed stirring things up. But what good it might do, he had no idea.

Sue Bright's studio, and Sue answered Johnny's knock. Her face showed first surprise, and then amusement. Inside the studio music played, a Schubert sonata. "A social call, lieutenant?"

"Not exactly."

"I could tell you that I am busy working. I am a working woman, lieutenant."

Johnny said nothing.

"On the other hand," Sue said, "a little interruption is sometimes good. Come in." She held the door wide.

Johnny walked into the large, pleasant studio. A fire burned in the corner fireplace. The music played on. There were photo floodlights carefully arranged, and two reflectors on stands. A Rolleiflex camera was mounted on a tripod. It was focused on the nude girl on the sofa who

132

made no move to cover herself, smiled happily at Johnny and said, "Hi.'

Sue Bright had closed the front door and was leaning against it, also smiling. "His name," she said, "is Johnny Ortiz. He's a cop."

"Far out," the girl said.

"A long way from Brookline, Mass.," Johnny said, and watched the girl's face change in surprise, in anger. "Your name is Jill." He looked at Sue. "She's your new bait?'

Sue's smile remained, but its quality was changed. "Meaning what?"

"To catch what you want to catch, when you want to catch it?"

Sue pushed herself away from the door. She walked to a table, took a cigarette from a box, lighted it carefully. She kept her eyes from the girl on the sofa. To Johnny she said, "Maybe you know what you're talking about. I don't."

He could smile then as he said in a tone of pure remonstrance, "Sue, baby." Pause. "Remember Tess?" Another pause. "Sent to bring Don Hastings in?"

"She's gone back to Daddy and Mummy in Texas."

"But I can bring her back," Johnny said, "any time I want to push the button." Not necessarily true; but he doubted if Sue was aware of the fallacy.

Sue said, "What do you want?"

Johnny looked at the nude girl on the sofa. "I wanted to meet Jill from Brookline. I've always heard that in Boston background was important, almost as important as breeding."

"Screw you," Jill said. She looked as if she wanted to move, but was not going to allow Johnny the satisfaction of seeing her discomfort; or discomfiture. A blush had begun between her breasts. It moved up her throat to her

133

face. "Drop dead," she said.

"Quite a vocabulary," Johnny said. " 'Far out. Screw you. Drop dead.' Finishing school, no doubt." He looked again at Sue. "I wonder what's in it for you. Besides the obvious, that is."

"When you find out, let me know."

"Oh, I will," Johnny said. "Believe me, I will." For the second time, the flesh of his back crawled as he walked out to the car. No rifle followed him this time; merely a glare of pure venom.

Last stop the automobile salesroom, and Billy Joe Harmon. "A cup of coffee across the street," Johnny said.

Billy Joe hesitated. The salesman friendliness was missing. He nodded shortly and walked over to speak to the switchboard operator. Then he walked out through the glassed-in doorway without looking to see if Johnny followed.

They sat in a booth, a formica-topped table between them. The coffee arrived slopped in the saucers, and both men automatically folded paper napkins as soppers. Johnny said, "You've been expecting me?"

"I reckoned you'd be along. You're not what I might call a friendly man, lieutenant."

Johnny shrugged. "Sometimes yes, sometimes no."

"The way I hear it, you leaned real hard on those boys. Now is that any way to behave?"

"I haven't even started to lean yet," Johnny said. He sipped his coffee. It was bitter, matching the taste in his mind. He set the cup down on the sodden napkin. "I don't like punk kids who lie to me," he said. "I don't like anybody who lies to me."

"You wouldn't be talking about me, now would you, lieutenant?"

"I don't know," Johnny said. "Have you lied to me?"

134

There was appraisal in Billy Joe's eyes, the look of a man in a poker game or a horse trade. There was resentment, too. But he tasted his coffee and said mildly enough, "Now just how did those boys lie to you, lieutenant?"

"A picture of Julio Romero," Johnny said. "They said they'd never seen him."

"And what makes you sure they had?"

Johnny smiled. "You can probably recognize the make and model of an automobile as far as you can see it, no?"

"Automobiles are my business, lieutenant. What does that mean?"

"Tracks are part of my business," Johnny said. "Romero's tracks were all around the horseshoe pit." Pause. "But the kids had never seen him."

Billy Joe took his time. He said at last, "I do believe I've heard of that, lieutenant, trackers who can follow a horny-toad down a dry paved highway, or a crow through the sky." He paused. "But I've never met one before."

Johnny sipped his coffee and said nothing.

Suddenly the salesman friendliness appeared. "Now why don't you tell me what you're really after, lieutenant? No sense you and me snarling and yowling at one another like a pair of tomcats on a back fence."

Johnny nodded. "Fair enough." And then, with no change in emphasis, "Do you know Sue Bright?" Long shot, of course, but he was playing hunches now. He watched Billy Joe's face.

For a moment Billy Joe was frowning. Then the frown cleared. "The photographer lady? I do have that pleasure, lieutenant. I bought some of her photographs ——"

"Nudes?"

Billy Joe's face saddened. "Now is that any way to talk? What I bought is what the lady calls her *photo-*

135

murals, pictures of mesas and mountains and the like, real pretty to look at." He tasted his coffee again. Over the rim of his cup his eyes did not leave Johnny's face; appraising eyes.

"Are you married, Mr. Harmon?"

"Billy Joe, now, please. And the answer is no. Never found a woman who'd put up with me for long. Maybe because I've sort of moved around, like a tumbleweed." His smile was broad and friendly.

"What would you say," Johnny said, "if I told you I think your boys, some of them anyway, are organized thieves?" He watched shock and incredulity appear in Billy Joe's face, overpowering the smile. "That," Johnny said, "the things they steal are pushed along south, mostly to Juarez?" He paused. "Maybe by you?" He paused again. "Maybe you've organized the whole thing?"

Billy Joe said slowly, in sadness, "I surely don't know where you get those ideas, lieutenant, I surely don't." He spread his hands.

Johnny said, "You knew Julio Romero, didn't you?"

Hesitation, almost imperceptible. "Why, yes, lieutenant, now that you mention it, I did. A fine boy."

"His father says he was a liar and a thief."

The sadness in Billy Joe's face deepend. "That is surely no way for a man to talk about his son, his dead son."

Johnny said, "We did a paraffin skin test on Julio's right hand. Not long before he was killed, he had fired a gun."

"Boys do, lieutenant."

"It could have been a particular gun, specifically a .357 Magnum Colt Python, the hand gun that killed Miss Lucy Carruthers."

Billy Joe was silent for a time. The sadness turned to

136

mild reproach. "Now, lieutenant, don't you think you're jumping in a little fast without looking first to see how deep the water is? What in the world connects Julio Romero, a fine boy, with Miss Lucy Carruthers getting herself shot dead?"

"His footprints there on the tiled floor of her house."

"I do believe he worked for Miss Carruthers."

Johnny nodded. "But not inside the house. Outside. And he didn't work for Cassie Enright, and his footprints were in her house, too."

"Are you looking for a scapegoat, lieutenant?"

Johnny shook his head. "Julio's dead. I'm after the man who killed him." Pause. "And I'll get him. He's a good shot with a high-powered .22. He's somebody Julio would listen to, somebody Julio would even take the trouble to meet out in the country if he was asked, or told. He's somebody who felt Julio was dangerous to him, too dangerous to be allowed to live." Pause. "Do you want me to spell it out for you?"

"I'd be right interested. I've always been fond of *de*tective tales."

Johnny was silent for a few moments, studying the man. He was good, he thought, very good indeed; if he was merely pretending relative disinterest, there was no indication of it in his face, in his eyes, in his voice, no small tell-tale hand movements, nothing. Well, all he could do was try. "All right," Johnny said. "It goes like this. Julio did the burglary of Don Hastings' house, while Hastings was kept away from the house in Sue Bright's company. Julio was a fool, and he couldn't resist that hand gun, so he took it. The Parker 16 gauge or the Browning over-and-under are worth more money, but to a kid who is brought up on TV, a .357 Magnum is the big deal." Pause. "You're with me so far?"

137

"Go on, lieutenant. Like I said, I'm right interested."

"Julio carried the gun," Johnny said. "It probably made him feel ten feet tall. But the trouble is, guns go off. He was carrying it the night he broke in to burglarize the Carruthers house. Miss Lucy should have been on her way to visit Mrs. Martindale out in Lejos, following a fake invitation, but she ran out of gas and walked back to the house to telephone for help. Julio was there. He panicked and used that gun he was so proud of." Johnny was silent, waiting.

"And then what, lieutenant?" Billy Joe's voice told nothing.

"Julio was a kid," Johnny said. "He was used to being told what to do. So he went to the man he trusted and told him what had happened, which was taking a big risk on his part." He paused. "But the man was smart. He did the best thing he could to cover up. He cleaned the gun, made sure it carried no fingerprints, gave it to Julio and told him to put it back in the gun cabinet where he had found it in the first place."

"Right under Mr. Don Hastings' nose?"

"You forget," Johnny said, "although I don't really think you do." His voice had hardened now. "You and Cassie went bar-hopping to find out where Hastings had been that night. So did I. He had been picked up by a girl named Tess, at Sue Bright's suggestion, and when the bartender wouldn't serve them any more drinks, Tess took Hastings not to his own house, but back to Sue's studio where he spent the night. Julio had all night to put the gun back in the cabinet as he was supposed to, and then the finger began to point at Hastings."

"*In*genious, lieutenant, it is indeed. I am impressed."

Johnny looked at the man for a long time in silence. "Then," he said, "a couple of things happened." His voice was soft. "After that bar-hopping, when Cassie found out about Hastings and Tess, and, more important, you both found out that I knew too, then the kids, Julio probably in command, were sent to work Cassie over — as a warning to me to lay off." Those night thoughts were running smoothly now. "That's the kind of crazy mind we're dealing with, the kind that thinks in terms of hostages and plane hijackings and bombs in public buildings. 'Leave me alone to do what I want, or I'll hurt somebody, anybody.' " He pushed his cold coffee away and rested both hands on the table. It was hard to keep them still. He watched Billy Joe steadily.

"Is there more, lieutenant? Because if there is, I surely do want to hear it." No faintest crack in the façade.

"There's more," Johnny said. "There's Julio Romero, who made the bad mistake of taking the gun in the first place, and the worse mistake of using it, and the worst mistake of all of telling the man about it, so now he was dangerous, because if I caught up with him, he'd talk." He paused. "Just as those kids at the shack will talk when I really start to lean on them." He paused again. "But Julio could talk about a killing, murder, and that would make the man an accessory to murder. So Julio was told to go out to a lonely arroyo to meet the man, and when he got there he was shot." A third pause. "Are you a good man with a high-powered .22?"

"Now, lieutenant, that's no way to talk. You've got a fine tight little story, and I surely would like to see it in the movie-films, but let's not be carried away." Billy Joe smiled easily.

"Then," Johnny said, "the final little touch, the thing that really started me in the right direction — planting those items in Don Hastings' house, probably while he was busy with Sue Bright and her new bait, Jill. Then the anonymous telephone call. And the statuette cut apart with the hacksaw — like Cassie's beating, pure threat to me." He shook his head. "I can see Hastings killing his aunt while he was stoned. Possible. But he didn't need to steal anything; he already had all he could want. And he would be the last man alive to mutilate his own statue."

Billy Joe said, "I'll be dogged if I've ever heard a finer tale, lieutenant, I will indeed. The folks out in Hollywood —"

Johnny had slid out of the booth and was standing now, looking down. "The tale isn't finished yet," he said. "Somebody is going to end up staked out on an ant hill. The kids will talk. Sue Bright will talk." He tossed a quarter on the formica table top. "The coffee's on me." He paused. "The ant hill will be on me too." He walked out to the police car.

Sitting on the corner of Tony Lopez's desk, "That's how it could have been," Johnny said. "It all fits." He paused. "But the hell of it is that I can't be sure."

Tony shook his head in slow wonderment. "At least, *amigo,*" he said, "you have stirred things up. I think you had better keep looking over your shoulder when you walk around."

20

Sue Bright drove her camper over Ben Hart's cattle guard, and stopped to admire the view. There was Cloud Mesa, one of her favorites, never twice appearing the same way. Today, now, its top was black because of a single cumulus cloud between it and the sun; yet its almost vertical sides were by full sunlight cast into bold relief. It was no wonder, Sue thought, that the nearby Pueblo Indians considered Cloud Mesa sacred, spirit-haunted, a living entity constantly reflecting its own moods.

As she watched, the cumulus cloud moved away, and the mesa top suddenly brightened. A good omen? She smiled at the concept as she put the truck in gear and drove on.

She loved this country and she had often thought that if ever she had to leave it, something important would go out of her life. There were those, she knew, who hated and feared its vast openness, which to her was its principal charm; and it always amused her to think that their dread arose from a sense of exposure, a belief that, in the presence of the great mountains and the limitless vistas, all of their secret thoughts and yearnings were somehow spread out in the sunlight for the world to see. She, Sue, could not have cared less who saw which of her secret thoughts and yearnings. She often told herself that she was what she was, and that was that.

She had married once. It was a mistake. She had wanted a whole man, or thought she had, but what she had gotten was a male *manqué* who tried to dominate her and failed miserably, and after that there was no point in even trying to preserve the relationship. Unmarried, she could do what she wanted, when she wanted, and with whom. It was much better.

She parked the camper by the main ranch house. As she got out, she looked admiringly at the glass wall; without even turning to look, she realized that it was oriented toward the great Sangre de Cristo Mountains, and she approved Ben's choice of view. Ben himself, bulky as a bear, came out on the portal as she climbed the steps.

"I'm Sue Bright, Mr. Hart. I'm a photographer."

"So I've heard." She seemed a nice enough female; maybe a little on the masculine side in jeans and worn boots, but, what the hell, Cassie wore the same, and there was nothing at all wrong with Cassie. Ben figured he was maybe a little out of date. So, credit where credit was due: "And a good photographer, I'm told."

"Why, thank you." Sue paused. "I wanted to ask your permission to take some pictures around the ranch, some of the buildings, some of the conservation work you've done on soil erosion in the arroyos, your stock tanks —" She paused again, smiling. "That kind of thing."

"Help yourself," Ben said. He looked down at the camper mounted in the truck bed. "That pick-up ought to get you wherever you want to go."

Cassie came out of the house to stand beside Ben on the portal. "Hi," she said. She had seen Sue around Arroyo Road, met her casually, knew her by reputation. Sue Bright and a girl named Tess, Johnny had told her, were Don Hastings' alibi for the night Lucy Carruthers was killed. True alibi, or false? Johnny hadn't known. Maybe another woman could find out.

142

Sue Bright said, "Hi." She was smiling still. "You're interested in the ranch too?"

"As a matter of fact," Cassie said, "I am." She looked up at Ben. "I still want to see that possible kiva." She looked again at Sue. Where was the harm, right here on the ranch? "If you give me a lift, maybe I could give you a hand with some of your work." Cassie paused. "Or maybe you're interested in what might be a new find."

Ben said, "Now look here, honey."

"Ben. Not Cloud Mesa this time. Right here on the ranch." Cassie smiled. "Promise."

Sue said, "I'd love to see it."

Ben raised his massive shoulders and let them fall. "Oh, hell," he said.

Sue drove casually and well. "How's Johnny Ortiz?" She glanced at Cassie's face for reaction. There was none that she could see. "He came to see me a couple of times," Sue said. She smiled. "Don't think I'm trying to be any kind of competition. It was strictly business."

Cassie nodded. "Tess," she said.

"You know about Tess?" The question was unconcerned. "She turned out to be sixteen. You wouldn't have known it. She's gone back to Texas." She turned off the dirt road and drove bouncing across open range land. "There's a spot over near the fence line I want to see. Okay?"

Cassie watched the distant mountains, sharp against the sky, and thought about Tess, sixteen years old, taking her fun where and how she found it. She said quietly, "Was Don with you that night?" She paused. "You and that girl?" Somehow the girl's name had become distasteful.

Sue glanced again at Cassie's face. "A morals crusade? Isn't that a little out of character?"

"I couldn't care less about your morals," Cassie said.

143

Not entirely true, she thought; and decided that she was lacking in scientific objectivity. "I'm only interested in where Don was."

Sue smiled then. "Not even in what he was doing?"

"Not even that."

"He was with us," Sue said. "Along about midnight he passed out."

"What time did he come to your studio?"

Sue's smile spread. "That's the question, isn't it? Where was he when the gun went 'bang!' up in Lucy Carruthers' house?" She turned to look again at Cassie's face. "Did you know her?"

Cassie nodded. Honesty strove with caution. Honesty won. "I didn't like her much."

"I don't know anybody who did." Sue paused. "Which makes all the fuss about her dying pretty silly, doesn't it? We kill how many each year on high-ways — fifty thousand? — and nobody does much about it. But one old woman who was thoroughly detested gets herself killed and we call out the National Guard." She looked at Cassie for answer.

"I don't quite see it that way," Cassie said.

There was that smile again, secret, enigmatic, faintly superior. "The difference between us," Sue said. "One of the differences." She paused, and the quality of the smile altered. "Maybe we should explore our differences one day?"

"I think not, thanks."

Sue shrugged. "Worth a try." And then, "Johnny?"

"Johnny."

"I tried it straight with a man once," Sue said, "wedding bells and all." She shook her head. "It didn't work." She was silent for a moment. "I'll give Johnny one thing," she said, unsmiling now. "He has *cojones. Muy macho.*" They were approaching the fence line now. Sue shifted

144

down, swung around a large piñon and a mass of sandstone boulders. "Here we are," she said, and stopped the truck.

Cassie said, "What — ?" And there the words ended. Her arm, resting on the window frame, was seized suddenly from outside the cab, turned, and bent backward until she thought her shoulder would dislocate. She screamed.

A voice almost in her ear said, "I'm right sorry about this, Cassie, but folks keep crowding me, and we've just got to make them stop." There was a sudden, pricking sensation in her triceps muscle. In a moment, "There now," the voice said. "Just rest easy." The arm was released.

Cassie drew her arm inside the cab. She rubbed the triceps area, and stared unbelieving at Billy Joe Harmon standing in plain view now, hypodermic syringe still in his hand. In only a moment the image of him began to waver in her vision as if distorted by rising heat rays. Suddenly it took great effort to turn her head to look at Sue.

"You aren't going to be hurt," Sue said.

"If," Billy Joe said, "that Indian *be*haves himself. If not —" He shrugged.

Sue said, "Now look, you promised ——"

"You look," Billy Joe said. "Just you behave your little self, and maybe nobody'll get skinned up." He watched Cassie's head begin to droop. Her eyes closed.

She tried to stay awake, and knew that she was going to fail. As if from a great distance she heard Billy Joe's voice again. "She's right near to out. Open the camper. We'll put her inside. You stay with her. I'll drive."

And Sue's voice saying, "Where are we going?" Was there fear in the voice? Impossible to tell.

"Never you mind," Billy Joe said. "You'll find out when we get there."

It was the last thing Cassie heard.

21

Ben Hart's voice on the telephone was an angry roar. "When she didn't come back," he said, "I got to wondering, and I took up the chopper to have a look. The camper's gone. There's a place where my fence has been cut, and there are tracks leading out to the road."

Had he known all along that it was going to happen, a kind of feeling in his primitive bones? Wise after the event, he thought with angry disgust. "I'll be right out," Johnny said. "Tell me where the fence is cut, and don't go walking around there."

There was a large piñon and a mass of sandstone boulders, a natural ambush spot. The four strands of barbed-wire fence had been cut cleanly and the strands pulled aside. Tire marks were plain.

Johnny walked carefully around the tire marks, and followed them back to the big rocks. There he stopped and stood for only a few moments studying the ground, finding all parts of the picture clear and plain. "The camper stopped here," he said, and pointed. A single drop of oil, round and sharp in the hard dirt. "A man was waiting. His prints are there and there."

Ben looked and shook his head. "I'll take your word for it. Do you know him?"

"No. But I will." A quiet voice. "Look there." Johnny pointed again. "They're deeper, and he's walking

146

with a shorter stride. Around there." He made a hooking gesture with his forefinger. "Where the back of the camper would be." He looked at Ben. "Do you see it?"

Ben said, "He was carrying something to put in the camper?"

"Something heavy," Johnny said. "Cassie." Still that quiet voice. "A woman walked around there, too, but from the other side of the tracks. Was Sue wearing boots?"

Ben nodded. "So was Cassie."

"They're not Cassie's prints." Johnny walked out to the police car. Into the microphone, "Call the MVD. Get the license number of a pick-up registered to Sue Bright. I want it found, held. A man's driving it, and he's dangerous. Tell everybody to watch it." He hung up the microphone.

Ben said, "I should have stopped her."

"You couldn't know." My fault, Johnny thought; nobody else's. He opened the car door. "I'm going back to town."

"What do you want me to do?"

A big strong old man, Johnny thought, just itching to get his hands on somebody, and God help the somebody if he did. "Get your fence fixed," Johnny said, "and then do the hardest thing of all — wait." He saw defiance in the old man's eyes. "They didn't take her for the fun of it," Johnny said. "They want her for a reason, and they'll be telling us what the reason is. She's leverage." God damn it, he thought, he was speaking of Cassie, Cassie! "They took her from here. They may call the house, you. Be there if they do. Then call me." He got into the police car and drove off.

Arroyo Road, strictly on a hunch. "I'm at Don Hastings' house," he told the microphone, and waited for no answer. He went down the steps to the patio at a half-trot.

Hastings answered the door at the second knock. He

147

looked sober enough, but the ferocious mustache lacked its earlier jauntiness. He looked at Johnny almost with resignation. "Now what?"

"Come over here." Johnny led the way out of the patio to the bare dirt at the side of the road. "Walk there." He saw hesitation and he dealt with it brutally. "I'm not going to tell you again. Walk!"

Hastings walked. Two steps, three. *"Basta,"* Johnny said. The footprints by the cut fence were not Hastings'. "Have you seen Sue Bright?"

Hastings said, "Will you tell me what this is all about?" Pause. "This seems to be my day to get my ass eaten out."

So? "Who else?" Johnny said.

"Cousin Lowell." Hastings wore a hangdog look. "He took Aunt Lucy's body to Boston and then came back. He's seen Jill."

"And he doesn't think much of you," Johnny said. "Neither do I. Now answer my question. Have you seen Sue Bright?"

"Not since the other night."

Inside the house the phone began to ring. "Answer it," Johnny said. "It may be for me."

It was. Tony Lopez said, "We've found Sue Bright's camper, *amigo."* His voice was gentle. "Empty. Left out on Tano Road." His voice was more than gentle; it was solemn. "The bed inside has been stripped." Pause. "There are bloodstains on the mattress."

The Sales Manager at the automobile agency said, "No, sir, Billy Joe isn't here right now, but I'll be happy to take a message. He —"

Johnny said. "Where is he, and what kind of car is he driving?"

148

There was a pause. "Mister," the sales manager said, "I don't know where he is, and as for what he's driving, we've got new cars and used cars and cars in the shop. We've got demonstrators and —"

"And you have records," Johnny said, "or ought to have for every one. Start checking, and when you find one missing, I want to know about it." He hung up the phone and leaned back in his chair, forcing himself to slow down, to try to think.

The footprints by the camper were not Don Hastings'. Scratch Hastings. Billy Joe Harmon then came immediately to mind, but Billy Joe was merely a guess. He had admitted that he knew Sue Bright because he had bought some of her photographs. Was there any more to it than that? Who might know? Someone who knew Sue Bright well, but not another man, not —

"I hope I do not intrude, lieutenant." Lowell Carruthers, neat and polite in one of his gray summer suits, polished black loafers, small-patterned bow tie. "I returned from Boston —"

"I heard," Johnny said. "Don Hastings said you ate his ass out." There was no humor in the statement. "I hope it took." He sat up straight. Of course, of course. "Sit down. Maybe you can help me. A girl named Jill, from Brookline."

"Yes, lieutenant." Carruthers sat down. "Her family and ours —" He shook his head. "I refuse to moralize. I spent my years in Paris after the 1914-18 war, and I daresay my behavior then was no more exemplary than Jill's is now." He paused. "What about her, lieutenant?"

"I don't think she'll talk to me," Johnny said. "But will she talk to you?"

"About what? Or whom?"

"Sue Bright and, maybe, Billy Joe Harmon. Cassie's

149

gone." He explained.

Carruthers listened quietly. He stood up. "Come along, lieutenant. We shall see what the young woman has to say."

Jill, barefoot, in jeans and the man's blue shirt hanging loose, answered the knock at the door to Sue Bright's studio. She was smoking a hand-rolled cigarette and the air inside the studio was heavy with pot odor. "You can come in Uncle L., but I don't want any part of this creep."

"I am afraid you have no alternative," Carruthers said. He walked past the girl. Johnny followed.

Jill hesitated briefly, and then closed the door. She looked at both men. "I'm going to get some kind of sermon? That I don't need. I live my own life ——"

"As you want to live it," Carruthers said in his quiet, polite voice. "I hope it works out for you, Jill. But that isn't why we are here. We want your help."

The girl inhaled deeply, held the smoke for a long time, exhaled with slow enjoyment. "That's a laugh," she said. "Out of sight. The only kind of help you'd want from me —" She gestured broadly and left the sentence unfinished. There was silence. The girl looked from one man to the other, growing curiosity plain. "What *do* you want?"

Johnny said, "Does Sue Bright know a man named Billy Joe?"

"How would I know?" The girl was smiling. "Next question?"

Carruthers said, "In the time you have known her, has Miss Bright mentioned any other man than Donald Hastings?"

The smile spread. "Don baby. That was a real gas when he showed up that night." She shook her head and the long hair flew. She brushed it back from her face.

"Who'd have thought, you know, that it would be some-body from home? Creeping out of my past? Pretty funny." The smile disappeared. "I guess you don't think it's very funny, do you?" She was speaking to Carruthers as if Johnny were not in the room. "What difference does it make? What's so special about us? Don baby, Sue, and me. So?"

"My question," Carruthers said, "was: has Miss Bright — ?"

"You've got it all wrong." The girl was smiling again, gesturing with the cigarette. "It isn't, you know, *Miss* Bright. It's *Mrs.* She was married once, isn't that out of sight? Sue, married?" She looked at Johnny. "How about that, fuzz?"

Johnny said, slowly, carefully, "Maybe she was just having you on."

"Not a chance. She just told me for, you know, laughs." Jill gestured to the picture rail. Nude photographs of herself had replaced those of Tess. "When she was taking those," she said. "See that one where I've broken up?" The nude figure was doubled over in laughter. "That was when she told me. And then to, you know, prove it —" She stopped. "Split infinitive, isn't it? Oh, dear, what would they say in Brookline?" She was laughing silently.

Carruthers said, "And what did she do to prove it?"

Jill inhaled deeply, stubbed out the tiny end of the cigarette. She exhaled at last. "You don't believe me, do you?" She was looking at Carruthers. "That's the trouble." She paused. "One of the troubles. You don't ever believe us. You live in your straight world, and you don't think anybody like me can ever tell the truth. Well, I'll show you." She walked across the studio with a curious, careful gait. She opened the drawer of a carved chest, pawed through papers, and turned at last in triumph. "Now what

151

do you say?" She waved a paper. "Her marriage license. Am I still a liar?"

Carruthers crossed the room slowly. "May I see it, Jill?" He took the paper from her hand and looked at it. Then he looked at Johnny. "Her maiden name," he said, "was Lettie Sue Harmon. I think your question is answered, lieutenant."

22

Once they knew where to look and what to ask, information came readily. "They're brother and sister," Tony Lopez said, reading from his notebook. "Born in Fort Worth, grew up in Waco. She went back to New York and got started in photography. She married Charles Bright in 1963, and she moved to Santo Cristo in 1965. She was already using the Sue Bright name professionally. Bright has dropped out of sight back in New York."

He turned a page of the notebook. "Nothing on her except the photography and a reputation for playing both sides of the *camino.*" He smiled suddenly. "Like the Anglos say, AC-DC." He consulted the notebook again. "Now the brother, Billy Joe, is something else. He's been up two, three times, but never taken a fall. Extortion, charge dropped. Assault, that charge dropped too. Impersonating a minister —"

Johnny said, *"Hombre!* You sure you have the right man?" And yet, he thought, it fitted at that; the man was an actor.

Tony said, "In El Paso he went around with a backside-to collar soliciting funds for a boy's club that didn't exist. Somebody hollered fraud, but that didn't come to anything either."

Carruthers said, "But I should say that it left Mr.

153

Harmon with the germ of an idea, don't you think, lieutenant?"

"El Paso," Johnny said, "Juarez just across the river." He nodded. "The shack. The boys." He nodded again. He felt no sense of elation that he had guessed right, only anger held under tight control.

"I wonder," Carruthers said, "if Mr. Harmon has ever read *Oliver Twist*. He appears to have copied Fagin rather successfully.'

Johnny said, "We'll get the boys in and lean on them a little, but they won't tell us much we can't guess already. Billy Joe set up the burglaries and made sure there wouldn't be interference. Maybe one boy at a time, maybe two or three did the actual work and delivered the loot back to him and he saw that it got to Juarez for distribution." He looked at Tony. "You have him living in El Paso at one time. Who were his friends? The El Paso police can work that end to find the fence."

Tony said, *"Seguro,* but —" He was silent.

"Understood," Johnny said sharply, allowing a little of the deep anger to show. "The kids and the fence in El Paso are secondary. Cassie's the main point, don't you think I know that?" Somewhere he had read the phrase *anxiety of helplessness,* and if anxiety could mean anger corrosive as an ulcer and increasing in quantum jumps as the sense of helplessness grew, then he knew exactly what the phrase meant.

"Amigo," Tony said. "Before we did not know who the man was. Now we can be sure. Even if we don't know what kind of car, we can set up roadblocks, stop and search everybody." He spread his hands. It was plain that inactivity wore on him, too.

Carruthers said, "You are thinking, lieutenant, that Dr. Enright is a hostage in the fashion that has become so distressingly popular these days — passengers held on hijacked aircraft in the desert? two officials kidnapped and one murdered in Montreal? the murdered West German diplomat in Latin America?"

It was exactly what Johnny was thinking, and had been from the moment he heard that Cassie was gone.

Tony said, "So they hit a roadblock and they have her with them, what do they do, shoot her? What good would it do? answer me that, *amigo.*"

It was Carruthers who said, "It depends upon the kind of mind you are dealing with, sergeant, and from what I have seen of Mr. Harmon and heard about him, I am not sure that he is at all real in the sense that most men are real and somewhat predictable. In our one brief encounter, I saw him as an eager salesman, a pious mourner, a wholesome reformer and philanthropist, and a very adroit evader of questions. His record shows that he is apparently capable of extortion, assault, and fraud; we know that he has used his sister's proclivities to maneuver Donald Hastings; we suspect that he murdered young Julio Romero; and we are quite sure that he has also committed the crime of kidnapping. Would you take a chance with a woman's life in the hands of such a man?" He shook his head slowly. "I am glad the decision is not mine." He looked at Johnny. "You have my sympathy, lieutenant; and, although I have no idea how I might be of help, my offer of every assistance."

Johnny nodded. "Thanks." A tough little man, he thought; not one to stand aside while others accepted responsibility.

"I am not being noble," Carruthers said. "Please understand that. I have a certain pride in my – background, lieutenant, and the members of my family and family friends who have been involved in these events have not showed in a very good light." He wore his faint, polite smile. "I will be happy if there is anything I

155

can do to alter the impression they have made."

Johnny thought of Tess and her parents, and of Julio Romero's patient, decent father. Now this one, trying to make amends. It took all kinds, even, apparently, Don Hastingses, Sue Brights, and, of course, Billy Joe Harmons. Friendly Billy Joe, politely escorting Cassie the length of Arroyo Road so she wouldn't have to bar-hop alone. You have him for a friend, Johnny thought, and you don't need an enemy. The son of a bitch.

The phone rang. Tony Lopez picked it up, spoke his name, nodded and handed it to Johnny. Ben Hart's voice said, "You were right, son. I had a telephone call. You better come out, because he'll probably call again."

"He?" Johnny said. "You recognized the voice?"

"He, she, it," Ben said. "Could have been anything, anybody." Pause. His voice dropped to an angry rumble. "But Cassie was there. She didn't sound good. All she said was, 'I really blew it, didn't I, Ben? I'm sorry.' "

"On my way," Johnny said. He hung up slowly, and sat for a moment controlling the anger arising from that sense of helplessness. He looked up at last. "I'm going out to Ben's ranch." To Tony: "You be here, available." To Carruthers, on pure hunch: "If you want to come along —"

"I do, lieutenant, I do indeed."

Don Hastings answered the knock and then stood blocking the doorway, scowling into the patio at Jill in her tie-dyed jeans and the loose-hanging man's shirt. "What do you want?"

"That isn't very friendly." Jill wore her dreamy half-smile. "The last time I saw you, things were, like, quite a bit different, don't you remember?" She paused, and the smile spread. "Old, you know, family friends."

156

"Beat it," Don said. "Buzz off."

Jill said, "Did the commodore lay it on you too? Is that why you're uptight? He put me down in his best quarter-deck voice. I expected him to point a finger at me and say, "Keelhaul that woman." She was smiling still. "He's kind of sweet at that."

"Cousin Lowell," Don said, "would cut your heart out and eat it for breakfast, on toast, if he took a notion to. Damn it, don't you understand? I don't want any part of you."

There was that smile again. "Because my family knows your family, is that it, Don baby? The old-school-tie bit? Isn't that sort of silly?" Her voice softened. "Besides, I don't at the moment have, you know, any other place to go."

"Where's Sue?"

"She gone."

"Where?"

Jill shrugged. "I don't know where or for how long, but I don't like staying alone."

For the first time he could smile and mean it. "Afraid of the dark? But it's still daylight."

"Funny man. Are you going to let me in?"

"Why should I?" And then, in a new, puzzled tone, "You don't scare that easy. What are you afraid of?"

"Not a thing. Why should I be?" Jill tossed her head, and then, automatic gesture, with both hands brushed back the long hair. Her eyes were steady on Don's face, too steady.

Don was frowning. "Is somebody after you?"

"You ask the damndest questions." Now her eyes were avoiding his.

"And I want them answered." Don paused. "Because," he said, "before I let you walk through this door I damn well want to know what I'm getting myself into. I'm already up to my ass in grief." He paused again. "Now what is it?"

"Nothing to do with you."

"God damn it!" It was almost a shout. "How do you know? Everything that's happened around here recently has had to do with me, and if it didn't, somebody sure as hell thought it did."

Jill brushed her hair back again. Her hands were not quite steady. "Why can't we just be, you know, friendly? Why be all uptight? You —"

Don said, and his voice was calmer now, solemn and determined, "You can take your pick. You tell me what's bugging you and let me decide if it has anything to do with me, or out in the street you go. I've been booby-trapped enough."

Hesitation; contemplation; a reluctant shrug. "Let me in," Jill said at last. "That's all I ask."

She sat, bare feet tucked up beneath her, on the bright Indian blanket-covered sofa. "You have any grass?" She watched Don shake his head. She sighed. "Then maybe a drink?" She waited in silence while he walked to the bar.

She held her drink in both hands, tasting it occasionally in sacramental sips. "I wasn't, you know, supposed to be there. I'd told Sue I was cutting out, moving on, too much to see and do, and too little time, you know, I'll be old soon enough." She sipped the drink. "But I hadn't gone, and I was maybe a little high, and Sue came back, but she wasn't alone."

Maybe true, Don thought, maybe not; with a chick like this you could never really tell. "Who was with her?"

"Some guy. I didn't see him. I stayed where I was, back in the bedroom. Then they came in, to use the

158

phone, and I went into the closet." Another sip, both hands holding the drink with care.

"For God's sake," Don said, "why? Why the big deal?"

"They had somebody else with them. A chick. She sounded stoned when she got on the phone, but I didn't like the way they talked to her." The girl's voice was not quite steady. "And somebody got slapped. I heard that." Her eyes searched Don's face. "A funny name. You know anybody named Cassie?"

The large room was suddenly still. Don said slowly, "I know somebody named Cassie." He paused. And I know Johnny Ortiz, too, he thought; and wished the empty feeling in his stomach would go away. "Go on."

Jill said, "The guy telephoned, but his voice sounded funny, like, you know, talking through a handkerchief with maybe something in his mouth?"

Don nodded. Mere acknowledgment. He said nothing. He watched the girl's face carefully.

"Somebody answered," Jill said. She stopped to sip at the drink. "Then they put this Cassie chick on, and all she said was, 'I really blew it, didn't I, Ben? I'm sorry.' That was when she sounded so stoned. Her voice was all, you know, mushy. Then they hung up."

Don got out of his chair. He walked to the glass door that faced the arroyo and stood there for a time, his back to the room. At last he turned. "What happened then?"

"I stayed in the closet." Another sip; the girl's eyes did not leave Don's face. "It was a long time. I don't know how long. I didn't hear anything, and so I looked, and they'd all gone back into the studio. They were talking, but I couldn't hear what they said." She paused. "I guess I didn't want to hear." She paused again. "And then Sue said, 'Look at this. The little bitch is still here!'" A third pause, remembering. "I don't know what she'd seen, and I didn't wait to find out. I went out the back way, past the carport, around that big wall – and came here." She was silent. Then, "I told you it didn't have anything to do with you."

"The hell it doesn't." Don hesitated. "The only thing is, I don't know what. Ever since that night, I've been walking in shadows." He shook his head. "No. Stumbling in shadows." He looked slowly around the room as if he were seeing it for the first time. "Stumblebum," he said in mild surprise. "I guess that fits. Remittance man, stumblebum. That goddam Indian. He and cousin Lowell, two of a kind."

Jill was watching him curiously. She sipped her drink, set it down for the first time, and brushed the hair back from her face. "Are you talking to yourself?"

Hastings walked over to the gun cabinet. He stood there looking at the polished metal and wood, the slim, lovely, deadly shapes. Over his shoulder he said, "You went out past the carport. Was there a car in it?" He turned to look at the girl. "Or was it empty?"

"There was a car. One of those, you know, little houses on a truck."

"A camper. Sue has a camper."

Jill shook her head. "This wasn't hers. A different color. This one is blue." She looked down at her drink. It was empty. She smiled in a vacant way. "Blue used to be my favorite color, did you know that? Long time ago. (In another life.)" The smile spread as she looked up. "I had a blue bathroom all my own, and a blue telephone in my bedroom. How about that?"

"Wild," Don said. "A blue camper."

Jill shook her head. "A blue truck. The – camper

was, you know, just metal colored." She paused, brushed the hair back and smiled again. "And it had a funny-colored license plate. I noticed that. Burnt-orange, not yellow like most." She leaned her head against the back of the sofa. "A little nap. You have ideas, they'll have to wait." Her eyes closed.

Don looked at her for a little time without expression, thinking of what she had said of a blue bathroom and a blue telephone. He knew the large house that had contained them. It was set well back from a quiet street, surrounded by lawn and tended trees, a rose garden, and a huge garage that had once been a carriage house. Well, the house he had come from had been of the same kind and quality. A long time ago, as Jill had said; in another life. What the hell.

He turned back to the gun cabinet, squatted to open one of the drawers. He hesitated only briefly and then took out the S&W .38 target revolver, swung out the cylinder and checked the five rounds it contained. He closed the drawer carefully, stood up, and tucked the gun in his waistband. A blue pick-up beneath the camper, he thought, and with burnt-orange license plate. That meant dealer plate. He had an idea he knew who was driving it.

Jill slept quietly, bare feet tucked out of sight, long hair partially covering her face. Hastings walked past her. In the hallway he took down a light wind jacket, slipped it on to cover the gun in his belt. He walked out then, and turned down Arroyo Road toward Sue's studio. A few Brownie points, he thought, might help his position with Johnny Ortiz and cousin Lowell. He had no idea what was going on, but bringing Cassie Enright out of it was certainly step one. As he walked down the road he felt better, easier, more his own man than he had in many days.

161

23

Old Ben Hart could not sit still. He heaved himself out of his chair and prowled the polished brick floor like a bear in a too-small cage. A very subdued Chico watched from beneath a table. "You think it's that automobile salesman?" Ben said. "How can you be sure?"

"We can't," Johnny said, "but he's our best guess. Cassie went off with Sue Bright. A man joined them. Billy Joe is Sue's brother, and all along I've been looking for somebody with the leverage to get Sue Bright to do the things she's done just when they were needed. Brother fits the bill." He was talking more than necessary, he knew, but it was either that or get up and pace the floor with Ben. Johnny glanced with envy at Carruthers, who sat quietly, legs crossed, watching, listening, not fidgeting a bit.

"Well, goddam it," Ben said, "what is there to do? Take the chopper out?"

Johnny shook his head. The old man wasn't stupid, just upset, more upset than Johnny had ever seen him. "We don't know what kind of car we're looking for, and we don't know where to start looking." He spread his hands. "Too much country. You know that, Ben."

Carruthers said, "Lord Nelson had a vaguely similar problem."

Ben stopped his prowling to glare at the little man. Johnny looked at Carruthers, too, opened his mouth and closed it again in silence. He said at last, "Admiral Nelson?"

"I don't think I have quite – flipped," Carruthers said. He wore his faint smile. "Nelson's problem was to find the French fleet and bring it to battle. With no telecommunications, no searching aircraft, only sailing vessels and his own intelligence. He pursued the French fleet, that is he hoped he was pursuing it, all the way across the Atlantic to the West Indies, and then back across the Atlantic. Eventually he met the French fleet off Cape Trafalgar, and destroyed it."

Ben said, "And what does that have to do —— ?"

Johnny said, "Wait a minute." He was studying Carruthers. "Go on. You're thinking what?"

"Mr. Harmon is finished here in Santo Cristo," Carruthers said. "Is that not so?"

"You better believe it," Ben said.

"And Billy Joe knows it, you mean?" Johnny said. He nodded. "He isn't stupid. So he's running?" He nodded again. "Where?" He ought to have seen it himself, but it bothered him not at all that Carruthers had guessed it first. All that mattered was that *someone* had come up with an idea. "Juarez," Johnny said. "That's the place that keeps coming up, isn't it? El Paso-Juarez, just across the river from each other. Friends to take him in, hide him."

"That," Carruthers said, "would be my estimate of the situation."

Johnny got out of his chair and walked over to stand in front of the glass wall. Behind the city the mountains towered green and white against the clear sky. He did not see them. He had a map in his mind, and he was studying it. "Three, four ways he could be going," he said, and

163

turned back to the room, "*if* he is headed for Juarez. Those are main routes. If he's sticking to back roads —" He shook his head.

Ben Hart said, "The international bridge going into Juarez. That's a real cattle chute, and he can't get away from it."

True enough, but Johnny didn't like it; the bridge ran from Texas into Mexico, both territories out of his jurisdiction. "Maybe —" He stopped there to look at Ben as the telephone began to ring.

Ben walked to it, picked it up, spoke his name. He nodded then. "He's here." He held the phone out to Johnny.

It was a voice Johnny did not recognize, indistinct, inflectionless, epicene. "A friend of yours here." There was a brief silence. Then, distinctly this time, "Johnny." Cassie's voice. "Oh, Johnny! Don — !" Sudden silence.

Johnny said, *"Chica.* Hello! *Chica!"* The silence held.

Then, "No roadblocks," the inflectionless, indistinct voice said. Pause. "Is that understood?"

Johnny hesitated. He took a deep breath. His eyes were on the mountains and the limitless sky as if somewhere in infinity he might find his answer. He said at last, "No roadblocks."

"A real good Indian," the indistinct voice said, and the line went dead.

Johnny dropped the phone in its cradle. He made no further move.

Carruthers said, "Safe conduct, lieutenant?" He nodded. "I see no other course — as far as the bridge at Juarez. How long will it take them to drive the distance?"

Ben said, "A little over 300 miles — five hours at least." He was looking at Johnny. "We can beat them with the chopper."

"No." Johnny stirred himself and shook his head. "Not yet."

"Tell me why." Ben's voice had rumbled down an octave.

"I'm not sure," Johnny said. Simple truth. Sometimes you relied on instinct, like a bat in darkness avoiding obstacles. And sometimes, he thought, instinct was wrong, too. But this time — "She mentioned Don," he said. "That has to be Hastings." He looked at Carruthers. "Why?"

"I have no idea, lieutenant. But I suggest that we —"

Johnny was already picking up the telephone, dialing a number. "Give me Lopez," he said. Then, to Tony, "Have somebody check Hastings' house. If he isn't there, find him." He paused. "And no roadblocks." And, damn it, he had almost forgotten: "And get to the automobile agency and lean on them. Hard. I want to know what Harmon's driving." He started to hang up.

"Oiga!" Tony said. *"Momentito!"* His voice became muffled, and another voice sounded indistinctly in the background. Then, clear once more, Tony's voice, *"Amigo,* a report of gunfire up Arroyo Road. We're checking it out." He hesitated. "You want to come in?"

Temptation was strong, but Johnny pushed it down. Here was where he could be reached, and instinct said that there would be another call. "I'll wait here," he said. "Keep me posted." He hung up. Waiting; as he had told Ben, the hardest thing of all.

The big room was still. Beneath the table Chico watched, motionless, as Ben walked over to the fireplace, picked up the trident poker, and began to prod savagely at a cold half-burned log. Carruthers sat quiet, legs crossed, one polished black loafer swinging gently. "Gunfire," he

165

said in his polite way, and shook his head. "You will persuade me yet, lieutenant, that this country of yours is indeed different not only in degree but in kind." He looked at one of the bold paintings on the wall. "A few days ago, I think I might have said that painting was an exaggeration. Now I am beginning to understand that the colors and the feelings are real."

The telephone rang. Johnny snatched it up. Tony Lopez's voice said, "We're still checking the gunfire, but Hastings isn't home. A girl who's been living at the Bright woman's studio is there, not making much sense. She says she doesn't know where Hastings is. He was right there talking to her when she went to sleep — or passed out."

"Okay," Johnny said, and hung up. He looked at Carruthers. "Jill is at Hastings' house." He waited.

"Indeed?" Carruthers' face had hardened. "She and Donald —" He paused, watching Johnny's face. "Yes, lieutenant?"

"Maybe she went there for a reason," Johnny said. "Hastings is somebody familiar, and if she wanted help of some kind —" He spread his hands. "I'm only guessing, but maybe she isn't just playing games."

Carruthers took his time. He said at last, "Thank you, lieutenant." He even smiled faintly. "I am not sure I expected compassion from you, but I thank you for it." He paused, and his voice turned reminiscent. "I used to take Jill, her brother, and Donald sailing out of Marblehead. Normal, proper, innocent children. Jill's brother is still normal, and proper, if no longer quite so innocent. Editor of the *Harvard Law Review* —" Carruthers shrugged. "I don't pretend to understand."

In the silence the telephone rang again. Johnny spoke his name. Tony Lopez said, "They've narrowed it down to three cars, *amigo,* all out on demonstration, and they don't

166

know which one Harmon has. A black sedan, four-door; a blue pick-up with camper; and a sports job, tomato red; all with dealer plates."

Johnny said, "I think we scratch the sports job. Sedan is possible, and the camper, of course. Put out descriptions, but we only want sightings, no stop-and-search, no roadblocks." He was silent for a few moments, turning it all over in his mind. "Okay, Tony. The best we can do." A big country, too big; too many back roads where not a single car passed in a day, two days. Sighting would be merely by chance, forlorn chance at that.

Johnny hung up and looked at his watch. Five hours of fast driving to El Paso. If and when he had to, he would ask for the bridge across the Rio Grande to be blocked, cars searched, especially black sedans and blue pick-ups with campers. But not yet. "I don't want them in El Paso or Juarez," he said aloud. "I want them out in the open."

Ben gave another savage jab with his trident poker. Carruthers said, "Understood. Open engagement with room for maneuver." He nodded. "Every naval commander's desire."

For the third time the telephone rang. Tony Lopez's voice was soft, angry. "We have found Hastings, *amigo.*" He paused. "Dead. You remember Julio Romero? It is the same. High-powered .22." Another pause. "Hastings had a gun in his hand, a .38, fired twice."

Men and rats, Johnny thought, the only species who destroyed their own kind. "Where is he?" The anger was hard to control.

"On the hillside behind the Bright woman's studio. The studio is empty and there is no car in the carport."

"Thanks," Johnny said wearily, and hung up. Still we wait, he thought, although the hunch was weaker now. He turned to face Carruthers. "Bad news," he said. You told it

167

straight out. There was no other way. A mad dog was loose, he told himself as he began to explain.

Carruthers showed nothing beyond a faint tightness at the corners of his mouth. "Donald," he said, "was an expert pistol shot."

Ben Hart, at last in a chair again, said, "Classic form of suicide. Man with a hand gun goes up against a rifle. On TV it works out. Other places it sure as hell doesn't." He heaved himself up again. "You want a drink?"

"Thank you, no." The Carruthers politesse was unshakable.

Johnny said, "If you want to go into town, Ben can have somebody drive you."

"No, lieutenant. Thank you, anyway. I have a personal stake in the affair now." His voice, still polite, held an edge. "May I ask what we are waiting for? I have revised my estimate of Mr. Harmon, and I am afraid that whatever happens, Dr. Enright's time is running out."

Ben Hart, on his feet, said, "Like a weasel in a hencoop, you mean? Kill everything in sight?"

Carruthers said, "I am not a psychiatrist, but I am beginning to believe that killing is Mr. Harmon's solution to all problems." He looked at Johnny. "What is your opinion, lieutenant?"

Johnny had been thinking the same, but he hated to say it aloud. "Roadblocks," he said, and shook his head. "Sometimes they work, and sometimes they don't. Usually you can see them a mile away and turn off or turn back, something. And they could be heading in any direction, even if Juarez is where Billy Joe wants to go." Then, remembering what Carruthers had said, "Where was the French fleet trying to get when it led Nelson all the way to the West Indies and back?"

Carruthers made a small nod of acknowledgment. "You have a point, lieutenant. Villeneuve, the French admiral, was trying to get into the English Channel without a fight in order to cover a landing from France."

"And Billy Joe," Johnny said, "might be running north or east or west in order to get south eventually, and we can't block all roads in every direction."

"Then," Ben Hart said, "just what in hell are you hoping for, boy? That they'll drive right up here and let us see just how good he is with that popgun? He —"

The telephone had started ringing again, and all three men looked at it. Johnny picked it up, spoke his name. The indistinct, epicene voice said, "No roadblocks? You're crossing me up, Indian. You want to hear the black girl scream? You get that fuzz pulled off, hear?" The phone went dead.

Johnny's fingers, he discovered, were not quite steady as he dialed his number; and his voice, speaking to Tony Lopez, was tight with anger. "I said no roadblocks. I meant it. Get them pulled off, goddam it, or —"

"We have no roadblocks, *amigo.*"

Johnny sat quite still.

"Amigo?"

"I'm here," Johnny said. Thinking, hoping, praying, he thought. He said slowly, carefully, "State Police. Ask them. Call me right back." He hung up, and stood quiet, staring at the distant mountains.

Ben Hart said, "What's doing?"

Johnny shook his head.

Carruthers said, "Perhaps a break, lieutenant?"

"Don't say it!" Johnny said. His voice was harsh. "Goddam it, don't even think it!" *Chica,* he thought, *chica,* we're trying.

The big room was still. Beneath the table the little

169

dog searched with his black nose for understanding, rolling his eyes from one man to another, his head motionless. When the phone rang, Johnny picked it up before the first ring was ended.

Tony Lopez said, "The only thing the State Police have, *amigo,* is a routine license and registration check." His voice was puzzled.

"Yes," Johnny said. He almost breathed the word. Sometimes the break, he thought. Not often, but sometimes, and this once was enough. "Where is it?"

"On the Las Lunas road, beyond Brand. But —"

"Basta!" Johnny said. The phone was silent while Johnny studied the map in his mind. "Okay," he said at last. "Call State Police. I want that license check packed up in fifteen minutes. Exactly fifteen minutes. Let the traffic move, and send the State cars on their way. Got it?"

Tony sighed audibly. "I guess so. But if you think I have any idea what you think you're doing —" He left the sentence unfinished. "Luck, whatever it is." He hung up.

We'll need it, Johnny thought, and turned back to the room. "Only one roadblock he could have seen," Johnny said, "and we know where it is, the Las Lunas road beyond Brand."

Ben Hart said, "Going north." He paused. "But it swings west, through the mountains —"

"Exactly," Johnny said, "and it runs into the north-south road through Cholla and on south to El Paso. How's your chopper, Ben?"

Ben was smiling, released from inactivity at last. "Let's go."

24

From the hillside above the parked camper, Billy Joe
watched the roadblock through his binoculars. There were
three State Police cars, cherry tops flashing, two on one
side of the road and one on the other. Three State cops
were stopping cars, checking them briefly, waving them
on.

That goddam Indian. If he, Billy Joe, hadn't been real
alert, he could have driven right up to that roadblock, and
then there would have been hell to pay and no pitch hot,
because if it was the last thing he did, and it probably
would have been, he would have gotten to that black girl
and seen to it that Johnny Ortiz never saw her alive again.

The trouble was, of course, that folks just wouldn't
stop crowding him, and he had never liked being crowded.
Then, too, there was that fool kid Julio Romero — what
was the saying: a tool that would turn in your hand? Well,
he sure God did just that, taking that pistol in the first
place and then pushing the panic button and blasting that
old woman who was silly enough to run out of gas. Times
like this, Billy Joe began to wonder if somebody up there
had it in for him, he really did.

What he had going with that shack and the two, three
boys in the know was a nice little operation that got
nobody skinned up except maybe the *in*surance com-

panies, and who cared about them? And then it had to go and blow up like a booby trap, all because of that fool kid, yes, and that goddam Indian Johnny Ortiz — and that brought him right back to the roadblock.

Something was going on. One of the cops had gone to his car and was hanging inside the window, probably using the radio, and what that meant, Billy Joe would just have to wait and see.

He glanced down at the camper. No sign of movement, which was the way it ought to be. Lettie Sue was good and scared of him, and she would see to it that the black girl didn't get herself untied and out of the camper. Lettie Sue had known from the time she was just a filly that her big brother meant what he said, and more than one time she had strap marks on her bare bottom to prove it.

Billy Joe had read a book written by some shrink once, and in it there was a female who had been *mo*lested by her daddy when she was real young, and after that she never did much like men, only other females. Sometimes Billy Joe had wondered, without regret, merely out of curiosity, if it was because of him that Lettie Sue favored other females over men, although he didn't really think so. Shrinks had funny ideas.

Shrinks talked, for example, about folks who didn't know right from wrong, and that was why they did things against the law. Well, Billy Joe didn't know about other folks, and he doubted if the shrinks did either, but with him it was pure and simple: right and wrong had nothing to do with it; in this world you were either a winner or a loser, and if you hankered to be in the win column, then you took what you could get because everybody else was trying to do the same thing. If folks would only understand that and stop crowding him, getting in his way, then

172

there wouldn't be any cause for all this trouble, no cause at all.

At the roadblock the cop had come back out of his car and was talking to the other two cops. Billy Joe watched carefully through his binoculars. One cop shrugged eloquently, turned to two waiting cars and waved them on. Then he walked over to his own car, flipped a casual hand at his fellows, got in and drove off, cherry top no longer flashing. The other two cops stood talking for a few moments and then they, too, got into their cars and drove off. The road was empty.

Billy Joe thought about it. Trap? Maybe, but he doubted it, he really did. In all this big country how could they know where he was? No, it almost had to be because of what he had said to that Indian, that the fuzz was pulling off all roadblocks, and as long as he had the black girl as hostage, the way was clear.

It was possible that they would set up something at the El Paso — Juarez bridge, he supposed, but he had ways of getting around that, too. There were places where a man could almost walk across that river. Let them find the camper, with a dead black girl inside; that would show them. And Lettie Sue? He hadn't made up his mind about her yet. At the moment she was useful. Later she might be a drag.

He had one last look at the road before he went back down to the camper. No cars in sight, just the ribbon of highway stretching into the mountains. He was humming a tune as he got into the cab, started up the engine and drove away.

The rifle was propped against the off seat within easy reach. And if by now they didn't know he was handy with it, then they didn't have the brains God gave a horny toad. That fool Hastings going up against him with a hand gun.

173

The world, Billy Joe had long ago decided, was filled with damn fools.

Cassie lay prone on the bare mattress of the camper bunk. Her hands were behind her, wrists tied with fine nylon cording she had long since given up hope of breaking. Her strapped ribs ached. Sue Bright sat on the bare bunk opposite, and when the truck engine started and they began again to move, she stood up to look out of the upper window without expression.

Cassie said, "You've spent how long building a reputation? Five, ten years?" At least her voice was no longer mushy, and she was thinking clearly again. It was not much, but it was something. "And you're throwing it all away, of course," she said. She tried to keep her tone reasonable, almost dispassionate. It was uphill work.

"I'll worry about that," Sue said. She sat down on the bunk again.

"You didn't think it would work out this way, did you?" Cassie said. "You were just giving the man a little hand, but things got out of control. One more killing."

"I think," Sue said, "that you'd better shut up. Billy Joe knows what he's doing."

"Of course he does. He's proved that all along. That's why he's running, and taking you along with him, leaving everything —"

Sue stood up, stepped across the narrow passageway, and slapped Cassie's exposed cheek viciously. "I said shut up, hear? Just you stop talking about him." She went back to her bunk.

There was something beneath the voice, the tone, Cassie thought; and she tried to concentrate on this, and forget her aching ribs and the painful cheek. "What if we talk about you instead?" she said. "Is that allowed?"

Silence.

With her head turned painfully, Cassie could look at

174

the other woman, study her. The camper began to sway as they started the climbing turning road into the mountains. "You're a good-looking woman," Cassie said, "pretty face, good figure, but you don't like men —"

"Do you want me to clobber you again?"

"No," Cassie said. "I don't enjoy it even a little bit." Pause. "Do you?"

Sue started to rise, and then sank back again. Her voice sounded weary, resigned. "No," she said. "That isn't how I get my jollies, if that's what you mean. I don't like the whipping bit, either giving or taking."

Was that a handle? "You've taken whippings?" Cassie said.

Sue's smile was without amusement. "Anthropological interest?" She was silent for a few moments. "Yes," she said, "I've taken whippings." Pause. "Until I screamed. Does that make you feel any better?"

The swaying camper; herself tied, helpless; Don Hastings dead; this wild conversation – the entire scene was unreal, but if she was going to retain any sanity at all and keep panic under control, Cassie told herself, she simply had to have something to concentrate on. A question had been asked; she tried to take it seriously. "It doesn't make me feel a bit better," she said. "Why should it? Do you think I enjoy misery, anyone's misery?"

"It doesn't matter," Sue said. "The whippings were a long time ago. They didn't leave any marks."

"But you remember them," Cassie said.

There was silence. The camper swayed on, running fast.

"So," Cassie said, "maybe they left marks after all. I know what it's like when you can't forget things."

Sue looked at her carefully then. "What kind of things?"

There was no need even to hesitate; the answer to that question was always right at hand. "Being black,"

175

Cassie said, "or half-black, which may be even worse, I don't know." She paused. "Being a fat little girl," she said. "I remember that, too, a black fat little girl and what the teachers called a gifted child to boot —" She waggled her head faintly. "A bad combination."

"You sound like a shrink."

"No." Cassie spoke slowly, distinctly. "I'm not a psychiatrist. At the moment I'm not even an anthropologist. I'm just a woman, hurt and scared almost out of her wits."

"I've told you," Sue said, "there's nothing to be scared of. We get across the border ——"

"You're wrong." Cassie could hold the tears back no longer, helpless tears, fear, panic close. She held her voice as steady as she could. "You're wrong," she said again, "and you know it. He's a mad dog. We've both seen it. He didn't have to kill Don, but he did. Just as he killed Julio Romero. You didn't know about that? Oh, yes. Johnny's known." She paused and took a deep, unsteady breath. The tears were hot on her exposed cheek. "He's going to kill me when I'm no longer useful alive. He'll do it just to hurt Johnny." Another pause. "And he may very well kill you, too. You're as afraid as I am."

"He's my brother," Sue said. Her voice lacked conviction. "Whatever he is, whatever he's ever been, he's my brother."

Oh, God, Cassie thought, I see it now. "But the whippings were his, weren't they? Weren't they?" She saw the answer written plain. "Until you screamed," she said, "and probably he didn't stop even then. There's no mercy in him. There's nothing at all. He's just the man with many faces and no heart, and you're – as – scared – of – him – as – I am!"

With three in the chopper, it was crowded. Carruthers was in the middle; Johnny, almost falling out the off-side, made himself as small as he could. He held two guns between his knees: his own rifle, and, snatched at the last moment from the police car at the ranch, just in case, a riot gun — a short-barreled 12-gauge pump gun loaded with buckshot. As they flew over the Las Lunas road short of Brand, Johnny made a clockwise circling motion with one hand and pointed to the west. He looked at his watch.

Ben swung the chopper obediently and checked his watch too. "We're cutting it awful close." Protest, but one look at Johnny's face and he gave it up. "You've got a place in mind?"

Johnny pointed. "Around Coronado Peak, there's a meadow hidden from the road."

Ben nodded. There was a stream in that meadow, he thought, and good fishing; one of the few places, all of them in high country, where you could find natives — cutthroat trout, some called them. Well, they were after different quarry this time, but maybe the word cutthroat was still apt.

He concentrated on his flying; just below timber line shaving the shoulder of Coronado Peak about as close as a man dared, and thinking as he did it that Johnny was probably right at that: the mountain itself would shield them from sight, and when they set down amongst the trees in that meadow they would be totally hidden from the road. And maybe, just maybe, with luck they could pull it off without somebody getting hurt. He wished he had a chance to spit over his shoulder; he never knew if it did any good, but he'd tried it a number of times and he was still alive and kicking, wasn't he?

Carruthers sat quiet, expressionless, watching the tree tops sweep past close; perhaps too close, he did not know. And when the trees opened suddenly beneath them, and a stream showed rushing through an upland meadow, he reflected merely that there was no substitute for local knowledge, none at all; whether it was a lobsterman's knowledge of every inch of a coastline and every rock and every current offshore, or knowledge men like these two had of the staggering variations of their own big country.

Here where Ben set the chopper down and immediately switched off the engine, the meadow and forest growth were as green and as lush as in the back country Carruthers knew so well two thousand miles away in Maine; and yet fewer than twenty miles by air from this spot, there was nothing but bare brown dirt, hundreds of miles of it, waterless, dotted only with chamisa and snakeweed and cholla cactus and sparse tan grass.

It was a savage country, too, he thought. In the space of only a few days he had lost two members of his family by violent death. It was a matter very much on his mind.

Johnny was out of the chopper before the rotor had stopped. He had his rifle and he ducked low as he started off. "This is mine," he said over his shoulder, and trotted across the meadow toward the trees and the hidden road.

The trees closed around him, and the air was suddenly chill. He carried his rifle in one hand at the balance, trotting steadily, working out the problem as he went.

Black sedan or blue camper, he could not know which he was looking for. But Billy Joe would be driving, that was almost a sure thing. And so Johnny wanted to be on the far, right-hand, side of the road where Billy Joe would be less likely to see him, because Johnny was going to have to make sure he had the right vehicle before he opened hostilities, and that meant that he might have to show himself a little in the trees. That was the first point.

The second point, more difficult, was precisely what he was going to do after he had identified and stopped the vehicle. It depended, of course. Billy Joe was armed, and well able to take care of himself with that high-powered .22 — as long as he could find clear shots; a bullet that small traveling at its enormous speed built a shock wave ahead of itself, and if it passed within a few inches of even a twig, it could be deflected. Still, this was forest country, with little undergrowth, and the deflection probability was diminished.

The kind of vehicle affected the situation, too. If it was the black sedan, then probably all three occupants — Billy Joe, Sue Bright, and Cassie — would be in view, and keeping track of everybody at once was going to be a problem.

But if it was the camper, then logic dictated that Cassie, and probably Sue as well, would be in back, and Billy Joe alone in the cab of the pick-up. Billy Joe first, Johnny told himself; that was the way it had to be. Then he could see what had happened to Cassie.

"Chica," He whispered it as he reached the road, looked both ways, and trotted across. *"Chica,* hang tight."

As he blended himself into shadow, rifle at the ready now, it occurred to him that little had changed in all the years since this was wild territory. Guns were still fired in anger and with intent; ambushes like this one were still laid; some men still took whatever they wanted to and could, and defied other men to punish them. It was no wonder that Carruthers looked around himself with astonishment. Johnny settled down to wait.

Faintly at first it came: the sound of an engine being pushed around curves and up a grade, the sound now plain, now muffled by trees, but steadily increasing in volume. It was coming from Johnny's left, the proper direction.

Johnny flipped off the bolt safety, and opened the bolt, drew it back only a fraction of an inch to see the brass of the cartridge in the chamber. Satisfied, he closed the bolt again.

Back at Ben's ranch, dialing the telephone for that penultimate call, his fingers had not been steady. Now they were entirely under control. His mind felt cold and

179

clear, hampered by neither hesitation nor doubt. The anger he had carried for what seemed an eternity was now banked and steady, a generative force. He waited, motionless, all impatience gone.

The laboring engine was closer now, only around the next curve — and then it came into sight: a blue camper. How many blue campers were there? No front license plate for identification, and sunlight reflecting from the windshield hid the face of the driver.

Johnny waited, motionless still. The reflections altered with the changing angles; the opaque windshield became transparent. It was Billy Joe at the wheel, no mistake.

Johnny waited until the vehicle was past him. Then he stepped out of the shadows, raised the rifle, and fired at the right rear tire. Automatically he worked the bolt, ejected the fired cartridge and slipped a new one into the chamber. There was no need for a second shot. The camper lurched as the tire went flat, and then began an uneven bumping as it slowed.

Johnny waited. He could not see the left door of the cab, but he was sure that it was opening and Billy Joe was coming out to inspect the damage, possibly, probably with rifle in hand. Johnny crouched and beneath the body of the pick-up caught a glimpse of a leg, a foot before it disappeared behind the left rear wheel. He was coming around the rear of the camper. Fine. Johnny raised the rifle, and then quickly lowered it.

The door of the camper had opened. Sue Bright had taken one step down, and was halted now, her mouth open in surprise, staring at Johnny. Beyond her, too close in the field of fire, there was sudden movement, across the road, into the shelter of the trees. Johnny crouched and ran toward the rear of the camper and around it, ignoring Sue, zig-zagging across the road.

180

There was a shot. He heard the bullet buzz angrily past his head, and close behind it the whiplash sound of the detonation. He ran, crouching still, dove over the top of a shallow bank, and rolled into the trees. For a few moments he lay still, listening. In the trees there were faint sounds of flight.

Slowly he got to his knees, glanced at his rifle and found it unfouled by the dirt. Slowly, too, he got to his feet, and at some distance in the shadows saw movement. Rifle at the ready, he started forward, tree-to-tree in short rushes. If this was the way it was, then this was the way it was, although he wished that it weren't.

Because the hunted had the advantage. He could pick his spot, choose his field of fire and his concealment, and wait. And if he was capable at the business, as Billy Joe had already showed himself to be, then the hunter was walking into trouble. But there was no other way; play it out now, or start the whole search over again.

Johnny moved on, tree-to-tree, shadow-to-shadow, and, as when he had turned his back on Don Hastings, the flesh between his shoulder blades was tight and prickling. The forest seemed very still.

Billy Joe had his spot. It was behind a lightning-felled tree, branches to shield him but not to interfere, a clear field of view forward and almost to either side. He had no idea how that goddam Indian had managed it, but here he was, and here, by God, he was going to stay, and rot.

In a way, Billy Joe was glad the man had a rifle in his hands, and seemed to know what he was doing, skittering amongst the distant trees, using light and shadow as camouflage, never pausing in full view for a careful shot. In a way it was better, more exciting, because Billy Joe had no doubts about how it was going to come out, he sure God did not. There were a lot of things he hadn't liked about the Army, but they had taught him to bide his time, and hit what he was shooting at, and a man couldn't really ask much more than that, now could he? He shouldn't really have thrown off that first shot; it was too hasty; but that was then, and this was now, and he felt calm and confident.

The figure in the trees was working closer now. Billy Joe watched, and was content. There, in a little clearing fifty yards away, a single big ponderosa offered shelter, and Billy Joe wasn't going to make the mistake of giving away his position before the man reached that tree. Or tried to reach it. He wasn't going to make it, that was for damn sure. At fifty-sixty yards he wasn't going to have a chance, not one.

Billy Joe settled the rifle against his shoulder, his cheek resting comfortably on the stock. He saw movement beyond the big ponderosa, and he smiled. "All right, Indian." He whispered the words. "Come on along. I'm waiting right here." His finger rested lightly on the trigger.

"Mr. Harmon."

The voice was behind him, quiet, polite, that little dude from the East. Billy Joe rose slowly, lowered the rifle from his shoulder, and held it loose and easy in both hands. He made no other move.

"Donald Hastings," Carruthers said, "was not very much, Mr. Harmon. On that I am sure you and I agree. But he was a human being, and he was also a relation of mine."

Billy Joe gathered himself. First this one, then the Indian, if that was how it had to be. From the sound of the quiet, polite voice, the dude was *di*rectly behind him and not more than ten, twelve feet away.

"Drop your rifle, Mr. Harmon."

Billy Joe smiled. "Whatever you say." He swung around suddenly with a dancer's speed, the rifle waist-high, finger firm on the trigger; and there was the dude, sure enough, just where he'd figured, neat summer suit, bow tie, black loafers and all, but unsmiling now. And he held a riot gun in his hands, which Billy Joe had not counted on, but it was too late to stop and there was no way to go but ahead. Billy Joe's rifle swung quickly. It was not quick enough.

The blast of the riot gun hurled him back into the branches of the fallen tree. The rifle fell to the ground. Billy Joe's body hung in the branches for a moment, and then slowly, almost blown apart, settled to the ground in a bloody heap and lay still.

Carruthers looked down at it without expression.

Johnny approached slowly, warily, his rifle at the ready. He came around the fallen tree and had his look. Then he looked at Carruthers.

"Police property, I believe, lieutenant," Carruthers said, and held out the riot gun, stock first. He ignored the body on the ground. "I told him to put down his weapon."

"I heard. I saw."

"I haven't decided yet whether I am sorry or content that he refused." Carruthers watched Johnny's face. "Do you wish to charge me, lieutenant?"

Johnny stood the riot gun against the tree trunk. So this was how it ended, he thought, or almost. One of his ancestors, Carruthers had said, was supposed to have quelled a mutiny single-handed with only his bare fists and a belaying pin. Johnny could believe it now.

"You have urgent business elsewhere," Carruthers said. "Attend to it. I will be here when you return." He watched Johnny nod and walk off, back toward the road.

It seemed a long way, Johnny thought, and reluctance, concern, worry made it longer. The forest was still again, the shattering echoes absorbed. Johnny had the insane feeling that he was alone in the world, and knew that it was merely an awful fear that prompted the concept. *"Chica."* Whispered again, it was a plea this time. He came to the edge of the forest and stopped, stared.

Sue Bright was lying at the foot of the camper steps, face down, the blacktop around her shiny and darkly red. She was unmoving.

Cassie, her hands still behind her, stood in the camper doorway. There were tears rolling down the sides of her nose; one side of her face was swollen, and a dried cut marred the other cheek. But she was erect, and steady enough. "Just the one shot as you ran past," she said. "I – heard it. And I heard it – hit her. It sounded like ——"

"All right, *chica,"* Johnny said. "All right. Easy." He was walking across the road, gun still in his hand, but forgotten now. Nothing mattered, he thought, nothing at all – but this. "It's all over, *chica,"* he said. "And you're all right." Through the tears she was trying to smile. "And so are you." "That," Johnny said, "was what I meant."